DANGER
THROUGH THE OAK
By Philippa Drakeford

*Credit must go to the Agency that told me that my illustrations
weren't 'fashionable' enough.
I was so annoyed, I went home and wrote this book.*

With thanks to Pat Mead for her help.

A Quirky Dragon Book
from Appleseed Press
Beyond the ordinary
- stories for young people by Philippa Drakeford

quirkydragon@yahoo.co.uk
www.appleseed-press.co.uk

First published in Great Britain 2010
by Appleseed Press, Essex, England
Printed in the UK

A catalogue record for this book is available from the British Library.

ISBN 978-0-9548572-9-5

CHAPTER ONE

"Does she *have* to come?" asked Rosie, round face screwed up in a grimace.

"You know what she's like, Mum," added her older half-sister, Rowan.

Jenny Meadows sighed. She was tired of her daughters complaining. She frowned and pressed her lips together, then announced, "Your cousin Holly is coming to stay and that's *final!*"

Rowan and Rosie rolled their eyes at each other. When Mum said things in that flat voice, there was no point in arguing.

Sighing, they slowly climbed the stairs, each footstep thumping like a reluctant elephant, up to their room where Cousin Holly would be sleeping. They had been ordered to tidy it up, before Holly arrived.

"I hate the way she spells her name with an 'i' at the end because she thinks it's cool," grumbled Rowan, gathering up books from the spare bed. They had seen it on the birthday card for their Dad - *To Uncle Robert luv Holli.*

"I hate the way she's soppy about her clothes," added Rosie.

"Yeah. *Fashion!*" Rowan put a weight of scorn into the one word. She walked over to the bookshelf and began fitting the books back in. She dropped one, picked it up, and looked at the cover: *Charm School*, by Anne Fine. It was one of her favourites.

"And she's sneery," said Rosie, half-heartedly picking up a sock that lay on the floor.

"And we're supposed to be nice to her!" Rowan wrinkled her nose.

"Why?" asked Rosie.

Neither minded being nice to people, but people like Holly…

"Because of Aunt Nadine and Uncle Roger getting a divorce."

"That was aa-ages ago. That was so long ago I can't remember!" said Rosie.

"It was ages, but not as ages as you think. I can remember," Rowan paused, thoughtfully. "We will try to be nice to her, anyway. I know it's difficult, but at least we'll have tried."

"Oh, all right then," agreed Rosie reluctantly. She picked up her toy crab, Sideways, and rubbed him against her cheek.

"I don't *want* to go," whined Holly. "I hate Rowan and Rosie. They're stupid and grubby and have no idea about fashion at *all*. Their clothes are all *totally* out of date, and they actually get some of them from charity shops, which is like, *so gross!* And they don't have Gurleez dolls, and they're not

2

interested in pop stars or anything cool! And they live in mud with loads of smelly animals."

"Don't worry, dear, you'll soon settle in," said her Mummy, applying lipstick. It was her Not Really Listening voice.

"*Why* do I have to go?"

Nadine Meadows sighed. "I've told you a thousand times. Your father is in Japan on business, and Gran and Grandad are on holiday in Provence, and I haven't got time off work, so my brother and your aunt Jennifer will be looking after you for the holidays." Nadine ran her own fashion business, and she was always busy. Holly's father was always busy as well.

Holly scowled. It wasn't fair! She didn't want to be shoved onto Uncle Robert and Aunt Jennifer, and she definitely didn't want to have to share a room with Rowan and Rosie!

Holly's favourite magazines were *Gurleez Gossip* and *Sweetie*. They were brightly coloured - mostly pink - and full of celebrity gossip, pictures of pop stars and adverts for glittery accessories, make-up and the latest must-have fashions. Holly read them avidly and then pestered her parents to buy her things. Her parents were divorced, which meant that if Mummy said no, she would whine, "But Daddy would buy it for me! Don't you love me best?" and if her Daddy said no, she would whine, "But Mummy would buy it for me! I thought I was your special little girl!" Then they would give in, and buy it. This strategy never failed.

Holly had her father's surname, Bostock, because they had been married when she was born, and, in fact, for most of her life. But then two years ago, they had announced they

3

were getting a divorce. "Won't make any difference," her Mummy had said cynically. "He's never here anyway."

"He is sometimes," Holly had muttered.

She had known her parents had quarrelled a lot, but she didn't see why they had to get divorced. She had felt a miserable, tight, angry feeling bunch inside her. It had stayed there ever since. Only a few things made it go away: when she'd just had something new bought for her, when she was wearing the most fashionable clothes of all the girls she knew, and when she daydreamed about being rich and famous and in all the magazines. She had to be a celebrity, so she had to know all the things they did, so she could do them too.

Holly was silent as her mother drove the four-by-four along the winding country lanes. It had been a long journey. Nadine had stopped three times to talk on her mobile phone, issuing instructions about her business. There had been traffic jams and roadworks on the motorway. Now the roads were narrow, with no pavements, flanked by hedgerows, tangled thorny brambles with dull green leaves and long pale brown dried grasses. Behind the hedges were fields, muddy grassy fields, with half-bare trees blowing in the wind, their brown leaves falling.

Finally, they drew up, and turned into a driveway, through the open wooden gate. Holly climbed stiffly out, looking down with dislike at the ground, wet, muddy, half covered with fallen leaves. So untidy! Autumn was untidy - even the sky looked messy, with a blustery wind blowing straggly grey clouds all over the place.

Holly's mother opened the boot, took out a suitcase, and carried it up the drive. With a sigh, Holly shouldered her rucksack (pink, fashionable) and followed her towards the whitewashed stone house. It had a wooden sign: Oakland Farm. It wasn't really a farm, hadn't been for years, but they kept chickens, she knew, nasty smelly pecking things. She could hear them clucking.

"They're here!" The door opened, and her Aunt Jennifer was there, red hair curling untidily about her face. "Hello, hello, come in!" She smiled, but Holly was determined not to smile back. She didn't want to be here at all, let alone be polite. They were ushered into the kitchen.

Uncle Robert appeared, and the adults greeted each other. Uncle Robert took the bags upstairs, and Aunt Jennifer opened the back door of the kitchen and called, "Rowan, Rosie, they're here, come and say hello!"

Rowan and Rosie appeared with polite faces. Aunt Jennifer put the kettle on. Uncle Robert reappeared, prepared to make conversation with his sister, but Nadine's mobile phone rang, so she stood in the corner, talking in clipped, businesslike sentences.

"Apple juice?" Uncle Robert offered.

"No thank you," replied Holly, coldly.

The three girls regarded each other with dislike. Holly had blue eyes, pink cheeks and long straight blonde hair like her mother. In fact their hair wasn't really blonde, it was brown, coloured blonde. Holly was thin, but worried that she wasn't thin enough. She wanted to be a fashion model, a pop star, a celebrity, and they had to be really *really* thin, else everyone

5

said they were fat. She was wearing her pink coat with fake fur trimming, and her pink frilled T-shirt with *Gurleez* on the front, and flared blue jeans with flowers embroidered on the legs. The toes of her pink and white trainers peeped out from under the ends of the flares, which were so long that they had scraped in the mud. But they were the height of fashion.

Rowan wasn't fat or thin, but never worried about how she looked. She had golden brown skin, green eyes like her Mum, and thick lustrous dark chestnut hair, which lit up as red as rowan berries when the sun shone on it. Her father, Taylor Rivers, was black - he and her Mum had split up after Rowan was born. Later her Mum had married Bob Meadows, Rosie's Dad and Holly's mother's brother.

Rosie was seven, four years younger than Rowan. She was a stocky, round-faced girl, with a tan over her pink cheeks. She had straight brown hair cut in a fringe, dark brown eyes, and a rosebud mouth, now set in a pout.

Looks like a gipsy, thought Holly scornfully.

Both girls were wearing jeans and knitted jumpers and muddy grubby trainers. Rosie had a woolly rainbow-striped hat to match her rainbow jumper; it was pulled low over her forehead, and her hair stuck out from under it.

Nadine ended her phone call.

"You will stay for supper, won't you?" said Uncle Robert.

"I can't, really. I have to get on," replied Nadine. They didn't look much like brother and sister - Bob Meadows's hair and eyes were dark brown, and his face and figure were round like Rosie.

Mummy can't wait to leave me, thought Holly bitterly.

Jenny Meadows glanced at Holly's tight face. "At least stay for a cup of tea."

Nadine agreed. The cup of tea was brief, as was the hug and kiss she gave Holly just before she left.

Holly heard the engine noise fade away.

That was it. She was stranded.

Bob shook his head slowly. "Nadine never stops, does she? I am so glad I gave up my city job. Lots of money, but no time. Working all hours."

"Good thing you did," agreed Jenny, "else you would've ended up with ulcers."

"High blood pressure," agreed Bob.

"A heart attack," said Rowan.

"A stroke," said Jenny.

"Gibbering fits!" grinned Rowan.

"Brain exploding!" Rosie put her fists next to her head, them flung out her arms. They all laughed.

All except Holly.

"Well," said Jenny in a bright voice, "Holly, why don't you go with Rowan and Rosie to see the garden and the guinea pigs?"

"Yeah, come on," Rowan invited, hoping her Mum was noticing the effort to be polite.

Holly's face said that was the last thing she wanted to do. She shrugged, and followed the girls.

They went through the kitchen door, out into the back garden. There was a stone-flagged yard there, a patch where herbs grew, and beyond that a lawn – although the grass

7

wasn't smooth, and was mixed with dandelions and clover. On the left was a vegetable garden, with a wooden fence round it. The rest of the garden was enclosed by a hedge.

"This is the garden," said Rowan, walking down the garden path, which was a series of stepping stones. Rosie hopped and jumped from one stone to the next. Holly mooched along sullenly.

"This is where Mum and Dad grow vegetables, and that's the herb garden, and this is the apple tree. Look, this is how you pick an apple," Rowan demonstrated. "You lift it gently, and if it's ripe, it comes off. This one isn't ripe. I can find you a ripe one, if you like."

"Don't bother," said Holly ungraciously.

Rowan sighed. It is difficult to be nice to someone who won't be nice back. "There's the blackberry hedge," she pointed out. "Only blackberry season is over."

On the other side of the hedge was a farmer's field, with clumps of ragged grass, thistles, dandelions and stinging nettles in it. There were large black and white cows grazing there. There was a gap in the far left hand corner of the hedge, and just a few paces from that gap was an old oak tree. The trunk and branches were bulging and gnarled, and the twigs made wriggly shapes. Some of the leaves were brown, others had fallen and lay scattered in piles. Holly thought the whole thing was horribly messy, and just typical of this family.

"That's our oak tree," said Rosie.

"Well, it's the farmer's really," corrected Rowan, "but the Robinsons don't mind if we climb it."

8

"It's a hollow tree, you can get in by crawling in that gap at the foot of it," said Rosie, "but you're not allowed to Holly, it's our private place!"

"Hush, Rosie," warned Rowan in a hiss.

"Wouldn't want to anyway!" retorted Holly angrily. "Crawling about like some kind of worm! I'd get my clothes all muddy, and I'm not interested in your stupid little secrets!"

"Good!" snapped Rosie, eyes blazing and cheeks red. "We don't want you!"

"Rosie!" said Rowan, although secretly she agreed with her sister. "That's rude."

"And I don't want *you*," returned Holly. "I don't want to be here. I'm only here because they *made* me."

There was an unpleasant silence.

Rowan sighed. "Well, as you *are* here, we've got to make the best of it. Come and see the guinea pigs, Holly." She caught Rosie's eye and mouthed, "Be nice. Her parents are divorced."

Rosie wrinkled her nose, rolled her eyes, puffed out her cheeks and sighed. Then she nodded.

Rowan smiled at her.

"Come on, Holly," said Rosie. "This way."

Against the wall of the house was a sturdy wooden guinea pig hutch. Squeaks and shuffles came from inside.

"This is Mohican and Pickle. Pickle's my one," introduced Rosie. Pickle was black, white and ginger, and her fur stuck out in all directions. Mohican was ginger and black, with just one splodge of white on her tummy. She was a rosetted guinea pig, which meant she had a Mohican furstyle,

9

sticking up between her ears. Both guinea pigs put their front paws on the wire front of the hutch so their furry bellies showed, and squealed, "Wheeple, wheeple, wheeple!" hopefully.

"Not food time just yet," crooned Rosie, then she changed her mind, darted over to the fence and pulled up a tuft of long grass from just in front of it. She fed it through the holes in the wire front. The guinea pigs snatched it eagerly and munched, their ears flopping up and down and the grass waggling in their mouths. "It's funny when they eat," giggled Rosie.

Holly was unimpressed.

Rosie unlatched the wire front of the hutch, reached in, and picked up Pickle, who went, "Wheep!" in protest, but, once held against Rosie's chest, relaxed.

Holly looked at her bright dark eyes and quivering pink ears, her funny whiffly nose, and fur that spiked up in all directions. She was cute, this guinea pig. But Holly didn't want to be pleased with anything.

"They like dandelion leaves," said Rowan. She walked to the lawn and pulled up a couple. "Would you like to feed her?"

Holly shrugged. "No," as though it was a stupid idea.

Pickle's head went up, as she sniffed the air and wheepled eagerly. Rowan gave a leaf to Rosie, who fed Pickle. Pickle chewed, the leaf whiffled around in her mouth, there were crunching noises and her ears quivered.

Holly refused to be charmed. "Dunno why you have to live here," she said.

"Why shouldn't we?" Rowan was kneeling in front of the hutch. She fed the leaf to Mohican, stroked her, then stood up.

"Uncle Robert should've stayed in the City like Mummy did. He was earning a lot of money," said Holly scornfully.

"He likes to be called Bob not Robert!" corrected Rosie.

"There are more important things than money," said Rowan loftily.

"Rubbish! Everyone wants to be rich and famous!"

"S'more important to be happy," said Rosie stoutly. She stroked her guinea pig. "I'm not rich, but I've got Pickle, and she's all furry, and I'm happy."

"Stupid guinea pig! She's a fat pig, just like you!" sneered Holly.

Pickle squeaked. "She *heard* you!" Rosie's brown eyes glared indignantly at Holly. She picked Pickle up, cradled her against her cheek, and rocked her.

"Course she didn't! She's only a stupid animal! She can't understand a word we're saying! Animals don't speak, thicko!"

"Oh, *don't* they?" retorted Rosie, eyes blazing. "Shows how much you know!"

"Sh!" Rowan's hand flicked in a quick warning gesture, and her eyes met Rosie's. Rosie closed her mouth and pouted, then, still cradling her guinea pig, turned and walked off.

"Now look what you've done," accused Rowan.

Holly shrugged. "So?"

Rowan sighed and gritted her teeth.

Holly walked inside, went up to the bathroom, and locked herself in.

"Supper!" called Bob Meadows.

Everyone gathered round the big wooden table in the kitchen. The kitchen was a large room, with a stone flagged

11

floor, and a stove in the big old-fashioned fireplace. The fireplace was a built-in alcove, with an old dark oak beam crosspiece. On the stove was a large iron casserole dish. Bob Meadows removed the lid, and fragrant steam curled out.

"Yummy!" sniffed Rosie enthusiastically.

Holly was not impressed. The food turned out to be some kind of stew, with beans, cabbage, potato and carrots, all in brown gravy with herbs. It smelt and tasted totally unfamiliar. "Probably fattening," she muttered to herself, picking half-heartedly.

"Aren't you hungry?" asked Aunt Jenny, concerned.

"No," Holly shook her head.

When the first course was finished – and Rosie had seconds - typical, thought Holly - Aunt Jenny put on oven gloves, and took a dish out of the oven. It smelt fruity and spicy. "Blackberry and apple crumble," announced Aunt Jenny.

Rowan and Rosie made eager noises. So did Uncle Bob. How childish, thought Holly.

"Holly, how much would you like?"

"That's not fair!" broke in Rosie indignantly. "Holly didn't finish her first course! You never let us have pudding unless we've finished our first course!"

Jenny felt uncomfortable. It was true of course, but… "Holly's a guest," she said firmly. "Holly, how much?"

"Er, a bit," said Holly. It was pudding, and probably fattening, but it did smell nice.

Rosie bubbled with annoyance like a small kettle. "S'not *fair,"* she muttered. She exchanged glances with Rowan.

The telephone rang. Bob went to answer it. A moment

later, he reappeared. "Rowan, it's your Daddy Taylor on the phone," he reported with a smile.

"Good-oh! Thanks, Dad!" Rowan bounded up from the table eagerly and went to talk to her father. After a few minutes, she came back, smiling. "Daddy Taylor's last gig went well. He says he's looking forward to next week."

"That's nice," smiled her Mum.

Holly could not understand why everybody was taking this so calmly. After all, this man had split up from Rowan's mother! And she had married *someone else!* And they were acting like he was a *friend* or something! There was none of that sharp scornful brittleness which was in her Mummy's voice every time she mentioned, 'your father'. None of that coldness which was in her Daddy's voice every time he spoke of, 'your mother'.

"Rowan's Daddy is coming over for Bonfire Night," Bob explained to Holly, in order to try and include her in the conversation. "He's bringing his drums and he's singing as well."

Holly lifted one shoulder in a shrug. Nothing to do with her!

"Daddy Taylor is brilliant!" Rosie bounced up and down enthusiastically. "You should hear him drum, he goes boom bom ba boom boom bom ba -"She began to drum on the table with her hands.

"Yes, all right, Rosie," said Jenny warningly.

Rosie stopped drumming but continued speaking, "And he goes all round the country doing loads of shows! Brilliant shows. We saw some, didn't we, Rowan? And," giving

13

Rowan no time to reply, "he wears special clothes, all colours, and the dancers are so beautiful, so he's doing that all over the country, and sometimes other countries, but he never forgets to phone you, does he, Rowan?"

"No," smiled Rowan. Then she realised that Holly probably didn't want to hear about how great Daddy Taylor was when her own father was in Japan and didn't ring her much or anything. So she said, "This is good pudding, Mum. Was it the blackberries we picked a couple of weeks ago?"

"Thanks," said Jenny. "I'm not sure. I just got some out of the freezer."

When they had finished – all of them had seconds except Holly - Rowan and Rosie had to clear the table. Jenny went outside to feed the chickens. Bob started running hot water into the large sink to do the washing up. They had two sinks, one for washing and one for soaking.

"We've got to go back, it's half moon," hissed Rosie, collecting bowls.

"I know," Rowan hissed back, stacking them, "But what do we do about Holly? We can't take her, can we!"

"She'd spoil it," agreed Rosie. She gathered all the spoons, and took them over to her Dad.

"Thanks," he said. "Holly's in the sitting room. Go in and keep her company, won't you? She's probably feeling homesick."

The girls rolled their eyes. "All right," agreed Rowan with a sigh.

CHAPTER TWO

Holly was in the sitting room, sitting on their comfy old sofa as though it was made of hard plastic, her hands clasped and her feet together.

"Hello," said Rowan.

"What d'you want?" demanded Holly rudely. Not even a telly! she was thinking. This place totally sucked! She had leafed through one of her Gurleez magazines, but she'd read it already.

Rowan was annoyed. She looked at Holly's magazine, Gurleez Gossip. It had photos of the Gurleez dolls, and their latest clothes. There was a blonde doll, a brunette, a red-haired one, and a black-haired one. They were supposed to be about eleven years old. All had pouting red lips, tiny noses, long eyelashes and vacant eyes. *We adore fashion – it's our passion!'* was their catchphrase. That, and, *'Gotta keep up with the latest!'* They never thought about, or talked about anything else.

Rowan and Rosie despised the dolls. They found them boring.

"This magazine's just one big advert!" said Rowan. "It just wants you to spend money buying new clothes for those stupid dolls!"

"They're not stupid! And it's not just an advert," snapped Holly. "It's got a picture story too! And celebrity interviews! It has all kinds of fashion tips on how to look good! You can buy the same clothes and accessories as your favourite Gurleez!"

"Wouldn't want to!" Rowan wrinkled her nose. "That skirt's so short and tight I wouldn't be able to walk in it, let alone run or jump or dance or climb trees or anything interesting like that! And those high heels would make it worse!"

"You're just babyish!"

"So are they – babies can't walk properly either!" retorted Rowan, and Rosie guffawed with laughter.

Holly went red with annoyance.

Rowan leaned over and read out some of the *Gurleez* magazine, "Treat your little sister by giving her a fab makeover to look like her fave star! She'll adore you for it!"

Rosie made realistic vomiting noises.

"This is saying you should give *six-year-olds* makeovers?" said Rowan incredulously, "That's crazy!"

"I wouldn't want to look like a soppy old pop star anyway,"

16

said Rosie. "They're all too thin and go all yucky and soppy over boys."

"You're just not mature enough," sneered Holly.

"It's not mature to wear lipstick and mascara and try and look like a teenager! It's immature! Anyway, Rosie's seven! She'd look ridiculous!" protested Rowan.

"I'm young enough to know better," said Rosie, rather smugly. "The only make up *I'd* wear is face paint to look like a tiger."

"Or a wolf," agreed Rowan.

"Childish!" snorted Holly.

Rowan held out both hands palm up. "We *are* children!" she pointed out.

Holly bent her head over her magazine and pretended not to have heard.

Rosie went over to her toy box, took out some wooden bricks, and began to set them up on the floor. She felt a bit sorry for Holly. Why couldn't she see that there were things much more fun than those boring Gurleez dolls? So she asked Holly, "Would you like to build too?"

Holly's lip curled in a sneer. "I'm not a baby!"

"Nor am I!" retorted Rosie angrily. She picked up a brick and placed it carefully on another one to make part of a wall.

Rowan took out pens and paper from the shelves in the corner, and started drawing a picture. She felt a bit uncomfortable because her parents had told her to be nice to Holly, not sneer at her magazine. Even if it was fluffy pink soppy rubbish. "You can borrow my felt tips if you like," she said politely to Holly.

"No. Drawing's babyish," snapped Holly. "Leave me alone."

Rowan shrugged. "Okay." She turned to her drawing.

Holly looked at them both, engrossed in what they were doing, completely ignoring her. She felt annoyed that they were ignoring her, then cross with herself for being unreasonable: after all, she'd asked them to leave her alone. Who needs them anyway? she thought, and got out another one of her magazines.

There were two pages of beaming celebrities, saying why they liked summer, 'because it's, like, so cool and fab,' and what they liked to wear best on the beach. And what not to wear on the beach, because it was, 'like, so last year.'

Holly wished it was still summer. Instead it was horrible muddy autumn, and here she was, stuck with her horrible muddy cousins.

After a while, Jenny came in and said, "Time for bed, Rosie."

"Aw!" protested Rosie, but she got up and packed her bricks away.

"What story would you like tonight?" asked Jenny as they went out of the door.

"Ummmm," Rosie was undecided. "Maybe Snow White – no, maybe Red Riding Hood… or the Firebird… or The Silver Apple?" Her voice, still reciting fairy tales could be heard as they ascended the stairs.

About an hour later, Bob appeared, "Time for bed, you two."

"Okay," said Rowan. "Look at my picture, Dad. It's a wood, see – and those are elves. And that's a hollow tree there."

"Oh yeah, you've drawn it in cross section so you can see inside. That's clever," said Bob approvingly.

Holly snorted. She was bored, and glad to be going to bed.

They went upstairs, and Rowan and Holly cleaned their teeth and changed into pyjamas.

The girls' bedroom was large and long, with two windows along the wall where the heads of the beds were. There were two cupboards, a very large and well-stocked bookshelf, and a table and chairs, all made of wood. There was also a doll's house, and even a rocking sheep, which is like a rocking horse, only it's a sheep, with real fluffy sheepskin sides. There were chime bars hanging from the ceiling, which glinted and made a faint tinkling sound. Rowan and Rosie loved it, but Holly thought it was babyish and unfashionable.

Rosie turned round when Rowan and Holly came in. She was snuggled down with her toy crab Sideways.

"Now, where's that book?" asked Bob, searching round the bookshelf.

"He's not going to read you a story!" exclaimed Holly in astonishment, sitting on her camp bed, which had been made up with a duvet and pillows and a sleeping bag underneath to be more comfortable.

"Yeah, why not?" frowned Rowan, climbing into bed.

"How babyish! Can't you even read for yourself?" sneered Holly in a pitying tone.

"Course I can read, dingbat! But it's nice to have someone reading a story aloud. We swap, Mum does me one day and Dad does Rosie, and then the other way round. And my Daddy Taylor reads when he comes to visit - well, actually, he tells. Without reading from a book at all. He knows lots of stories, Anansie stories and African stories about the clever tortoise, and sometimes he sings songs." Rowan smiled. "It's cool. Don't your parents ever read to you?"

"Course not! Wouldn't want them to, I'm much too grown up!" snapped Holly.

But she kept glancing at the way Rowan snuggled up to her step-Dad as they both sat on the bed and he opened the book. "Now, where were we?" Then he looked up. "You can listen too, Holly, if you like."

"Yeah, it's a good story, about elves and things," invited Rowan, who had decided to make another effort to be nice. "I don't mind you sitting on my bed either."

"No thanks," replied Holly ungraciously, and turned her back.

But she couldn't help hearing the soothing rise and fall of Uncle Bob's deep voice, and the way he made the characters come alive, and a wistful part of her thought it would be nice to have Mummy or Daddy read to her…

But they can't. They're too busy with work. And I'm too old for that stuff really, she told herself.

All the same…

Holly was woken up by a rustling and whispering. She opened her eyes, then hastily half closed them so that nobody would know she was watching. Rosie and Rowan were out of bed! And what's more, they were getting dressed when it was still the dead of night. "I can't wait to see them all again!" Rosie was whispering excitedly.

20

"Sh! You'll wake Holly. She mustn't hear," warned Rowan. "Pity we have to go tonight."

"But it's a half moon! It's the only night we can go!"

"I know, I know. We'd better take some sandwiches, just in case."

"Okay."

Holly watched them dress and creep out, and close the door behind them. She listened to their furtive footsteps. Then she sat up in bed. So, Rowan and Rosie were sneaking out! And their parents didn't know! They were bound to get into trouble if somebody was to tell on them... and they wouldn't be so smug and superior then, would they? Holly smiled, enjoying the feeling of power. But in order for it to be a really convincing story, she would have to follow them, and find out what they were up to.

Quickly, Holly slipped out of bed and pulled on her flared jeans, her top, and her socks and trainers. She ran a brush through her hair and tied it back with a pink scrunchy. She tiptoed to the door, and slowly opened it. It creaked.

She winced and froze, and listened, but could hear nothing except the wind blowing outside and rustling the trees.

She crept downstairs, stair by stair.

Perhaps she was too late, and they had already gone? The house was strange at night, with unfamiliar shapes and shadows. Her hands were clammy and her heart pounded. Carefully, carefully, she unhooked her coat, put it on, crept to the back door and opened it. It was unlocked - that meant Rowan and Rosie had gone through it.

Outside, it was even scarier. Her vision fizzed in the grey-black night. In the sky was a white half-moon, with clouds scudding across it. Everything felt very big and strange, and it was all so dark. Holly was used to orange street lights. But she could just see the dark figures of Rowan and Rosie, progressing down the garden with a cross between a tiptoe and a dance. There were muffled giggles, so they were obviously excited.

An owl hooted and Holly jumped. She watched them push through the hedge, and followed them with long, quiet paces. What on earth were they up to?

Then, to her amazement, they ducked down, lay flat on their tummies and first Rosie and then Rowan slid on their elbows into the gap at the foot of the hollow oak tree. Holly watched the soles of Rowan's boots wave as she disappeared into the tree.

But the strangest thing of all was that the gap in the tree was not dark, as would be expected. Instead there was a light coming from it, a greeny golden light, like morning sunlight shining through leaves.

Holly suddenly realised she was standing only a pace away from the tree, and staring. What was she to do next? She had no intention of lying down on the ground and getting her clothes all muddy, but the more she looked, the more overwhelmed she was with curiosity. And if she bent close, she could actually hear something... it sounded like birdsong.

Before she knew what she was doing, Holly was down on the ground. She stuck her head into the arch, and crawled towards the beautiful light that dazzled her eyes. Her trainers were the last to disappear into the tree.

And then the garden and field were dark and silent once more.

CHAPTER THREE

The first Rowan and Rosie knew about it was a loud squeal. They whirled around and saw that most unwelcome of sights: their cousin. Standing there, mouth and eyes wide with astonishment and fear.

"What are you doing here?!" shouted Rosie angrily. "Go away!"

Holly recovered enough to say, "Oh yeah? And what would your parents say if I told them you were out of bed in the middle of the night?"

Rosie clenched her fists and muttered dangerously. Rowan put a restraining hand on Rosie's chest. "Okay, you're here," she said wearily. "I suppose you can come along with us.

But it's secret, all right? You're not to go telling anyone! Promise!"

"What is this place anyway?" demanded Holly, without promising anything. "How come all this fits inside a tree?"

"This is Nuin Duir," replied Rowan. "It's another world."

"It doesn't fit *inside* the oak tree, stupid!" said Rosie. "The oak is a doorway! It's magic!"

"I don't believe in magic!" retorted Holly.

Rosie threw up her hands. "Use your eyes, stupid! How else did we get here?"

"Rosie, don't call her stupid," said Rowan.

"Why not? She is," muttered Rosie.

"Look," Rowan tried to speak calmly. "Holly. This is a land we found, the oak tree is a doorway into it, it's called Nuin Duir, we've been here before, and we're going to meet some friends of ours. We can stay here days but when we go back through the oak to our world again, it will only be a few minutes after we left. So Mum and Dad won't even know we were gone."

"Unless *you* tell them, and you better not!" put in Rosie.

"You can stay here," continued Rowan, "or you can come with us."

Holly wrinkled her nose up. "Stay *here?* You want me to stay here in the middle of some messy, muddy wood? I don't *think* so!"

Rowan shrugged, and started off through the wood again. Rosie turned and followed. Holly paused helplessly, not knowing what was best. Then she started after them.

They were making their way along a grassy, earthy path in

25

a forest. Trees of various kinds were growing either side of the path. Most of them were either oak trees with their rough craggy bark, gnarled branches, and distinctive lobed leaves, now a russet colour; or ash trees with greeny-grey bark, their leaves yellowing from green. Bunches of seeds - ash keys - hung from their branches. There were also slender silver birches with white bark and lemon yellow leaves and, to their right, the ground sloped upwards into a patch of beech trees like tall grey pillars, in amongst glorious leaf colours of crocus gold and caramel golden brown. There were bushes too, hazels with hazelnuts, hawthorns red with berries, wild roses with red rosehips the same shape as the rosebuds that had been there in the spring. The leaves rustled in the fresh autumn breeze, birds sang, wood pigeons cooed, insects buzzed, and there was the mushroomy leafy earthy frosty smell of a forest in autumn.

Rowan and Rosie strode ahead happily, enjoying the sounds, scents and sights. Holly trailed behind, whining, "My jeans are all muddy. My trainers're muddy. I bet this'll never come off. It's spoilt."

"So are you," muttered Rowan.

After they had been walking for about ten minutes or so, there was a scuffle, a rustle of leaves and something dropped out of a nearby tree and straight into Rosie's arms. All three girls jumped. It was a roundish creature with beautiful silvery-grey fur, round ears, a long tail, whiffly whiskers, little paws and very bright eyes.

"What is *that?*" demanded Holly.

"Misty!" exclaimed Rosie, her face lighting up.

26

"Rosie, Rosie, Rosie!" chirped the creature happily. "Hello, hello, hello!"

Holly's jaw dropped. "It can *talk?!*"

"Course. See, I *told* you animals can talk and you didn't believe me! I *told* you so!" Rosie stuck out her tongue at Holly.

"Rosie," warned Rowan. Rosie just pouted.

"Rowan, Rowan, Rowan! Hello, hello, hello!"

"Hello, Misty!" Rowan reached out a hand and carefully stroked Misty's soft fur on her head.

Holly wrinkled up her nose. "What *is* it?"

"She's a chinchilla," said Rowan, annoyed at Holly being so rude.

Misty looked at Holly with bright black eyes. "Who this sourpuss? Got lemons on her tongue? Eh? Eh? Eh?" she asked in her high pitched chittering voice, holding her head on one side and whiffling her whiskers. Rowan and Rosie couldn't help giggling.

"Looks like a rat! Keep it away from me!" sneered Holly.

"This is Holly, our horrible cousin," said Rosie loudly.

"Rosie! Don't be rude!" said Rowan.

"Why not? *She* is!"

"Holly, Holly, Holly! Hello, hello, hello!" Misty walked along Rosie's shoulder and stuck out her nose to sniff.

"Eurgh! Keep off!" whined Holly. "Get it away, it's probably got fleas!"

"Fleas? No fleas, don't worry, worry, worry, Holly, Holly, Holly!" squeaked Misty.

Holly didn't reply, just wrinkled up her nose and took a few paces backwards.

Misty's eyes widened, very deep and black and shiny. "Did I say wrong?" she asked Rosie in a rather pitiful voice.

"No you didn't!" retorted Rosie. "It's just her, being horrible! Ignore her!"

"Oh! Well, you got a hazel nut, Rosie? Yum, yum, crunchy, crunchy!"

"No, 'fraid not."

"Tut tut tut! Pity!"

Holly marched off behind a nearby tree, feeling angry. She leant against it, then realised that the tree was covered in this green powdery stuff, which must've come off on her clothes. She groaned. She hated this place, but she wasn't sure which was the way back.

"Rowan! Rosie!" This time it was another voice calling, a musical voice. From between the trees appeared a slender person, with golden brown skin, white-gold hair and green eyes.

"Linden!" called Rowan happily.

The person ran up to them, as graceful as a gazelle. She was an elf, just a little taller than Rowan, and she was wearing a long tunic made up of heart-shaped lemon-yellow leaves. Round her waist was a belt woven from thin strips of bark. Her feet were bare, her ears were pointed and her leaf-green eyes almond-shaped. "Rowan! Rosie! I thought I heard you! It's good to see you again!"

"You too!" agreed the two girls and they hugged each other. They were so happy that they quite forgot Holly.

"Wonderful news, is it not?" asked Linden excitedly.

"What news?" asked Rowan.

"You mean Misty hasn't told you?"

"Sorry, sorry, sorry! Misty total scatterbrain sometimes!" Misty hid her face in her paws.

Linden shook her head with a mixture of affection and exasperation. "Never mind. It's truly wonderful news! Our troubles will soon be over – the Three are here!"

Troubles? Rowan wondered what was going on, but before she could ask, Rosie spoke:

"The Three?"

"You remember, Linden mentioned it last time," said Rowan. "The Maiden, the Mother and the Crone!"

"Oh yes, them! I remember!" cried Rosie.

"Will we get to see them?"

"Oh yes, they want to see you in particular!"

"Really? Ooh, I feel a bit nervous about that," admitted Rowan.

"Don't worry," advised Linden. "Just come with me to the Sacred Grove. Lots of us are there."

Holly watched Rowan and Rosie walk away with Linden, Rosie with Misty on her shoulder. Unhygienic, thought Holly. But she was curious to know what was going on, and who these Three were. So she followed them through the wood, until they reached the Grove, a circle of trees and bushes. Holly didn't know one tree from another, but there were twelve kinds of sacred trees there: Yew to the left of where the people were entering the Grove, followed by Silver Birch, Rowan, Ash, Beech, Willow, Hawthorn, Oak, Holly, Hazel, Linden, Apple and finally an old stump, covered with Ivy to the right of the entrance.

There were lots of other elves like Linden, some of whom were greeting the girls, and there were more chinchillas, squirrels, deer, and birds as well.

And, in the centre, three women, the Maiden, the Mother and the Crone.

Rowan and Rosie were urged forward by Linden and the other elves.

"I got butterflies in my tummy," admitted Rosie, catching Rowan's eye.

"Me too," whispered Rowan. But they put their shoulders back, and walked forward.

The Maiden had hair that fell in waves like a waterfall, palest silvery gold, bright straw-gold, saffron yellow-gold, and copper-orange mingled. Her skin was creamy pale, except for her rosy cheeks, and it was sprinkled with honey-golden freckles. She wore a robe that was made out of white blossoms, May blossom and roses and snowdrops, as pure and crisp as a cloud in the summer sky. Some of the petals had just a hint of pink, apple, pear and cherry blossom. Her rosy mouth looked as if it was made for laughing and rejoicing, and her eyes that seemed to be sky-blue one minute and pool-water green the next sparkled with delight. Rowan thought she was like the Spring Maiden they had seen the second time they came to Nuin Duir, only this Maiden was solid, not made up of sparks of green and gold.

The Mother reminded her of the Mother of Autumn that they had witnessed earlier this year in the Autumn Equinox Dance, who, like the Spring Maiden had also been made up of sparks, this time golden and orange and red. This

Mother was solid too. Very solid. She was a huge, magnificent woman, both tall and broad, as solid as a hill or a great tree. Her skin was as brown as a chestnut, and she wore a robe that was red, many shades of red: blossoms as bright crimson as blood, wine red roses, leaves the colours that Virginia Creeper goes in autumn, orangey red, dark red, almost maroon like copper beech. Her hair was wavy, in wriggles of black and chestnut and deep red. Her cheekbones were broad, her full-lipped mouth glad, and her dark brown eyes glowed with a loving gladness. Her lap was made for curling up in, her strong arms for cuddling, her chest for resting your head against.

The Crone was tall, thin and upright. Her straight deep black hair, with a streak of grey and white in the middle, fell about her shoulders. Her face was partly hidden by the black hood of her long black robe, and she wore a cloak of black crow feathers that had a greeny-purply iridescent sheen on them. Her skin was wrinkled, tanned with time. Her hooked nose like an eagle's beak jutted out between her prominent cheekbones. She had a narrow-lipped shrewd mouth, and a determined chin. Beneath arched black eyebrows were deep-set eyes, very dark. Their colour was mysterious – was it actually black, or just a very dark brown or dark purple? You couldn't tell, but there was a spark in them that told you she would brook no foolishness, that she was wise and expected the best of you whoever you were. She could look grim, and she would be tough, but the crowsfeet round her eyes told you that she would also laugh, and understand.

31

Just being in the presence of these Three would send a tingle of excitement and joy through you, make you feel as though you had swallowed sunshine. Indeed, as the Mother let out a huge glad laugh – a laugh that shook her whole body like a small earthquake – and held out her arms, Rowan and Rosie ran joyfully towards her, and scrambled onto her lap. She hugged them and rocked them and welcomed them, while the Maiden skipped and danced round, singing, and the Crone looked on with a glow in her dark eyes. The Maiden smelt of jasmine blossom, the Mother like roses and apples, and the Crone like earth and incense. Rowan and Rosie both knew that they would always remember this moment.

But why didn't Holly run forward too?

When she first saw the Three, Holly's heart gave a great leap of excitement.

Then she thought: Why am I feeling like this? She knew it was no good feeling excited about anything. If you started to feel excited and happy, people let you down, just like Mummy and Daddy did.

Holly looked at the Mother and said to herself: Huh! She's *fat!* She needs to go on a diet, all that floppy flesh. A diet probably wouldn't be enough. She'd need to have all the fat sucked out of her, and her stomach stapled.

And the Crone is so *ugly!* Her nose is hooked and her chin is pointed and her skin is wrinkled and her hair is grey. She needs a facelift, and a nose job, and botox for her wrinkles. She needs lots of plastic surgery, and hair dye. And I bet

32

she'd still look ugly!

The Maiden's hair is messy, and she's got bare feet with dried mud on them, and she's too curvy, not nearly thin enough, and her nose is the wrong shape, and her eyelashes are too pale, she needs mascara. And she's got freckles. There can't really be anything special about people who are too fat and too old and too messy. There isn't *really* anything special about them at all.

Holly couldn't understand why they looked so happy and confident when they were so ugly, especially the Mother and Crone. If she were that ugly, she'd just *die!* She didn't want to see beyond the way they looked. And the more she thought about how they looked all wrong, the more she shut out the specialness, and the duller and uglier they seemed.

Stupid, the way they're all crowding round, making a fuss, she said to herself. I don't want to be a part of this.

She looked all round, but nobody was paying any attention. So she began to back off a little, and then she wandered away, all the time thinking about how this was a strange place, and she wasn't sure she liked it, and her jeans were all muddy. Was there such a thing as a place with a shower here? It was rather like a fairy tale, so perhaps there was a fairy tale palace with a princess, and luxurious baths, and perfumes and gorgeous clothes and things. That would be the place for her, not this messy dirty wood and all these animals and hippy-type people. She mooched miserably along for several minutes.

There was a sudden screech. Holly jumped, looked up into a nearby tree and saw a bird, which screeched again. It was reddish brown, with a streak of blue, and she assumed it was a pigeon because it was the same size. In fact it was a jay, and its cry was a warning.

"What's a pretty girl like you doing here? You don't belong in a place like this, I can tell."

Holly jumped again. An elf was standing there, looking at her with his head tilted slightly. Like the other elves, he was slender and only slightly taller than she was. Unlike them, he was wearing a sleek silver and black outfit, trousers, knee length boots, a jacket, and a wide belt. His skin was silvery-white, and so was his hair.

"I'm looking for somewhere better," she said, flattered.

"Somewhere you belong? I'm Nexus, by the way."

"I'm Holly."

"Cool name. Tell me, Holly, have you ever been to the Mall before?"

She smiled. "The Mall? As in shopping? As in clothes?"

He grinned back, white teeth in his silver-white face. "As in the latest fashions! As in the coolest ever shops! And did you know we're looking for trainee models?"

"Really?" she asked eagerly.

"Of course! I can just tell you've got potential!"

"How do I get to be one?"

"Come with me to the Mall and you'll see."

Just for a moment she hesitated. What about Rowan and Rosie? What about never going anywhere with strangers? But that was strange *men*, she told herself. Nexus wasn't a man, he was an elf… and he was so nice! And she could be a model! Like she'd always wanted to be! Now she was here, she may as well enjoy herself! She beamed. "Lead me to it!"

So he led her through the trees to a clearing, where there was something similar to a car, only rounder, like a silver egg with a black screen. He pointed a gloved hand towards it and pressed his thumb on a button on the palm of the glove, and a door slid open with a hum.

"OMG, that is so cool!" exclaimed Holly.

"Ah, if you think this Pod is cool, just wait till you see the Mall," said Nexus, gesturing for her to climb in.

She did. The seats were black plastic fake leather, and very comfortable. A seatbelt moved across to strap her in. Nexus sat next to her, pressing buttons. The screen lit up. The door slid shut. The Pod hummed, and Holly felt her stomach lurch a bit, like being in a lift. The Pod flew.

The screen did not show what was outside as a window would, instead colours represented the landscape features, such as hills, and the dome of the Mall. Nexus talked entertainingly of what awaited her there. Holly planned to boast to her cousins big-time once she got back and saw them again. But she wouldn't hurry. She would enjoy herself first.

They landed, and the door slid open to show that they were on a high platform, overlooking the town inside the artificially lit dome of the Mall. Holly gasped with excitement. She couldn't stop looking at everything as they stepped into a transparent glass lift, which slid elegantly down an equally transparent glass lift shaft.

There were tall buildings, blazing with colours, and huge advertisements for clothes and accessories and cars and shares in companies; mechanical voices boomed and persuaded and cajoled people to buy buy buy. The inhabitants walked with a strange mincing swaying gait, and wore the most colourful extraordinary extravagant clothes that Holly had ever seen, and their hair was piled high and teased and twined into fantastic hairstyles. All had the same silver-white skin as Nexus.

"There! The models." He pointed to a screen. As the camera panned across a row of ladies, so slender and silver and elegant, decked out in the finest clothes, they moved, swayed, put a hand on a hip, tilted their heads, turned, walked… and the sound of applause rang in Holly's ears, both from the screen and from the people on the streets, who were exclaiming:

"Look, look! See the new look!"

"Oh, we must have it now!"

"They look fabulous!"

Holly was aching to try something on. "Can I go to the shops too?"

"Have you credits?"

"Er, no," she admitted.

"Then you can't buy anything. Besides, I'm taking you to the model school right away. I was under the impression that was what you wanted. To be a model."

"Oh, of course! Sorry! And thanks!"

He inclined his head gracefully. "Not at all. This way."

Two elf girls saw her, and stared. "Look at *that!*" said one.

"What does she think she's doing, coming out without skin-cover?"

36

"And what *is* she wearing?"

Holly blushed. It's not my fault! she wanted to say. I got muddy in a stupid muddy wood with my stupid muddy cousins! Then she thought: Just you wait till I'm a model! I'll show you!

CHAPTER FOUR

Meanwhile, Rowan and Rosie were joining in the celebration, and meeting their friends again. As well as Linden, there was Beechen the Beech elf who had golden-brown skin, golden hair and light green eyes. The leaves of his tunic were in autumn golds, like crocuses and caramel. Everyone was talking and laughing and joking while Misty rushed up and down, along people's arms, bouncing off their heads and shoulders, chattering excitedly and asking anyone if they had any hazel nuts.

38

The Maiden threw up handfuls of blossom which fell like snowflakes all around. People laughed, running it through their fingers, then the Maiden began a hopping skipping dance, and suddenly everyone was grabbing each other's hands to form a line, following the Maiden in loops, up and down, winding around the trees, while little birds swooped and dived in and out of the dancers, chirping a joyful song. The elves began to put words to it. Rosie said: "It sounds like Green Grow The Rushes O!"

"Yeah, it does," agreed Rowan, and they both joined in, although the words were different.

"I'll sing you three, O!

Green grows the forest, O!

What are your three, O?

Crone, Mother, Maiden!

Two, two, the Goddess and god,

There to balance us out, O!

One is one within itself, and ever more shall be so!"

"Any hazel nuts, O?" sang Misty, and everyone laughed.

"A fine idea! Let us eat!" the Mother's deep glad voice sang out. Everyone paused in their dancing, rather breathless and red in the face, but still fizzing with excitement. The girls thought it was like being at a birthday party with lots of games where you run around having fun - and then it's time to eat!

The Mother approached an apple tree and touched it, and suddenly apples swelled all over the branches. "It's an honour, Mother," beamed the elf in charge of the tree, who had a round, chubby, apple-cheeked face, and green eyes.

Several elves went forward to help gather the apples.

Then the Mother went on to a cherry tree and a hazelnut bush, and a twining briar rose which produced red rosehips. She gathered them in her hands, pressed them together, opened her hands and there was a chalice of wood, brimming with a deep pink liquid.

"What's that?" asked Rosie.

"Rosehip syrup," replied Linden. "It's delicious! Would you pass us a mug, Beechen?"

"Of course," Beechen tilted his head politely. Suddenly wooden mugs were everywhere, and the elves were toasting each other and the Three, and lifting the mugs to drink. The rosehip syrup was sweet and tasted a little of roses and a little of fruit.

The Maiden held up her hands and sang to the bees, and they came down from the sky, buzzing happily.

"Is that safe?" asked Rosie. "Won't she be stung?"

"Sting the Maiden? Never! Bees are her special creatures," said Linden.

The bees settled upon her outstretched palms, then she cupped them together, and when she parted them again, the bees flew away, and there was a perfect globe of honeycomb. The Maiden broke it in half so you could see the hexagons of wax and the deep golden honey dripping out, and then she passed it to an elf who popped a piece in her mouth, and declared: "Delicious!" then began to hand it around.

The Crone meanwhile, bent and tapped the ground with her staff and mushrooms sprang up, popping out of the ground. Elves ran forward to gather them, and from beneath her cloak the Crone produced a black cauldron. She tapped the ground with her staff again and a little fire sprang up, its golden flames crackling merrily. She placed the cauldron on top, the elves threw the mushrooms into it, and there was soon a hissing and spitting and the wonderful rich scent of frying mushrooms.

The meal was delicious. People passed things around and made sure nobody went without, everybody had a leaf as a plate, piled with juicy fried mushrooms, crunchy hazelnuts, crisp scented apples, and sweet juicy cherries, washed down with rosehip syrup, and followed by sweet golden nuggets of honeycomb.

Rowan was licking honey from her fingers, when she frowned, looking around at the circle of elves and realised someone was missing. "Hey," she said, "Anyone seen Holly?"

"Oh!" Rosie's eyes grew wide. "I forgot all about her!"

"When did you last see her? It was before we saw the Three, wasn't it?"

"Yeah. I think the last time was when we met Linden."

"Oh." Rowan sighed. "She might be in trouble. We'd better look for her."

"Oh, she's probably just sulking somewhere!" said Rosie impatiently. "She'll be all right."

"What if she isn't? She could've wandered off and got lost."

Rosie sighed deeply. Her lower lip stuck out.

"Misty, have you seen Holly anywhere?"

Misty blinked. "Holly Holly Holly? Your horrible cousin?"

"Yes, that's right."

41

"The one who said I probably got fleas - ick, itchy scratchy!"

"Yes, that's her."

"Have you seen her?"

Misty blinked her large shiny black eyes again. "No."

At that moment there was a general shushing, and it wasn't just the breeze in the leaves of the forest. "Hush, hush, the Three are going to speak!"

The Crone stood, and held out her arms. Everybody was silent, looking at her.

"Friends," she began, "Inhabitants of the forest, we have rejoiced, and that is right, we have eaten, and that is right, we have shared and laughed together and that is right. But we are here for a purpose more solemn than that, and the time has come to talk of it. To talk of the trouble that has come to this land of Nuin Duir, the trouble that is causing such sorrow and suffering."

There was a general murmuring, heads nodding, people whispering.

"Who wishes to speak and bear witness of what they have seen?" asked the Crone.

Several people rose.

"I'm going to have to say something," hissed Rowan.

"But it's the middle of the meeting," objected Rosie.

"I know. But every minute matters. If Holly's lost, or in trouble, we have to tell them." Rowan took a deep breath. How embarrassing, to have to stand up in front of everybody and admit that they'd lost their cousin! And not just in front of their friends, but in front of the Three, the Goddesses, the special sacred spirits who never came without a particular reason.

But she stood up, and looked at the Crone. The Crone's dark eyes gazed right back at her. Rowan swallowed. She twined her fingers together, then rubbed her sweating palms against the sides of her jeans.

"What have you to say, Rowan Rivers Meadows?" asked the Crone.

Everybody turned and stared at Rowan.

Holly was awed by Zantia, who was in charge of the model school. She was so slender, the way her cheekbones stuck out and the shadows under her cheeks, lined with a silvery-blue makeup on the silver-white of her skin!

Oh, if *only* I was that thin! I would do *anything* to be that thin! Holly was so busy thinking things like that that she wasn't paying attention to what Nexus was saying - something about having found her, and her having potential. They were in Zantia's office, which had a shiny desk, some slender-legged chairs made of thin metal bars, a computer, and a television screen on the wall, broadcasting images of models and the latest fashions.

"Excellent, Nexus," approved Zantia. "Two hundred credits for you, with an extra five hundred if she makes the grade."

"Thank you, Zantia," Nexus tilted his head gracefully. "I must leave now. Good luck, Holly."

"Thanks!" Holly beamed. Nexus left, closing the door quietly behind him. Holly twined her fingers together nervously as Zantia scrutinised her with silvery-blue eyes…

was she wearing contact lenses? Holly wasn't sure.

"So, you wish to join us."

"Yes please!"

"For what purpose?"

"To be a model! I've always wanted to be a model!"

"How much do you want it?"

"Ever so much!"

"How much do you know about how our system works?"

"Er... not much." She didn't want to admit to knowing nothing at all.

"We have a system of credits here. Everyone needs credits in order to buy the latest fashions. Oh, and food, of course. Credits are earned, while you are at school, by passing all the necessary tests. Those who leave school must get jobs, which is how they earn their credits. Those who fail must pay the penalty - the penalty for pupils here, of course, is expulsion from the school."

"I'll pass!" said Holly, determinedly.

"Ye-es," mused Zantia. "Stand."

Holly stood, while Zantia walked all around her, high heels clopping on the black shiny floor of the office. Holly felt uncomfortable being judged like this.

"Well, the first thing we shall have to do is get all that ghastly filth off you," said Zantia.

Holly blushed. "Sorry. It's from the wood. I'm normally very clean. I have a shower every day, sometimes more than once."

"I'm sure you do. But you must get rid of those dreadful clothes."

Holly cringed. She wanted to protest that her clothes were very fashionable - but of course, she told herself, here the fashions were different. They tended towards padded shoulders, nipped-in waists, and trousers with tight ankles.

"You need a new outfit, of course. We shall provide you with one, which means you shall be in debt to the sum of fifty credits. And the make-up you use in lessons will be another ten. But if you pass your tests, that debt shall of course be repaid, and you shall gain credit, which you may start spending immediately."

"Thank you!" Holly's eyes gleamed, with visions of being able to go to all those cool shops and buy whatever she wanted passing through her mind. All those fabulous outfits… all the girls at school would be so jealous if they knew! And she'd be bound to be able to take some back with her when she left here… but she would stay for as long as she could. It was going to be beyond amazing to be a real model!

Holly was clean and sparkling all over. She had showered, had her hair cut and styled, and was wearing an entirely new outfit: magenta tights, a bright pink tight-fitting long-sleeved T-shirt, over which was a jacket with wide padded shoulders, and long drooping sleeves, with a bright purple plastic belt to tie round it. Finally there were the high heels, also pink. She should have been feeling on top of the world, but she wasn't.

It was her classmates. None of them were friendly. Each of them glared at her, sizing her up as competition, then made unkind remarks:

"Look at her ears! What happened to them?" All of them had pointed ears.

"She's so big-boned!"

"Her nose is quite wrong."

"Her feet are enormous!"

"She is so not elegant!" They had all tittered, showing bright, tiny little teeth.

It had been the same all through the lesson in make-up, where Holly's face was covered with the same silvery-white stuff they all wore, then she practised putting on mascara and eyeliner and lipstick - which she would have enjoyed, had they not been so horrible to her.

And it was even worse in the walking lesson - Holly had felt herself quite graceful, she had been to dancing classes and so on, and practised walking like a model, but it was much more difficult walking in these shoes. The heels were higher than the ones she was used to, and they weren't platform heels, which were fashionable back home. These heels were spindly cones. Her ankles wobbled. She wobbled. She stumbled and tripped, and fell over, and they all laughed - not loud roarings, but with elegant tinkles.

"Such a creature! I've never seen anything like her before!"

"Where was she dragged from?"

Holly didn't know which of them was worse. She thought it was Vectira, until Zarifa started to talk, but then Karina was even more nasty... it wasn't always easy to tell the difference between them, all of them seemed to be trying to look the same, to fit the same pattern.

I'll show them, Holly thought. I won't give up, I won't!

CHAPTER FIVE

"So you have no idea where your cousin Holly is?" asked the Mother.

"No," admitted Rowan. "She must've wandered off."

"I bet I know what's happened." An elf with creamy-white hair stood up. Her name was Meadowsweet. "I bet she's been taken by one of them from the Mall."

"Yes, they take people sometimes," agreed other elves. "And animals. They capture animals."

"They kill them and use their skins for their clothes."

There was a gasp of horror. Misty squeaked and jumped into Rosie's arms, buying her head in Rosie's chest. Rosie cuddled her, "Don't worry, Misty, I won't let them take you!" she declared. Her brown eyes met Rowan's green ones, both of them deeply shocked. As elves stood up to speak to the

48

Three about the Mall, and what went on there, they became even more shocked.

"The elf Thistle volunteered to go to the Mall and try and find out more, and stop them," Meadowsweet told the gathering.

"She got in all right. We heard a couple of reports from her."

"She told us that they never see the sun inside the Mall, or feel the rain on their faces, or touch the earth. But then the reports stopped coming," continued Meadowsweet. "So the elf Holly decided to go."

Rowan and Rosie had time to think what a coincidence it was that there was an elf Holly as well as their cousin Holly. But then, Holly was one of the Sacred Trees in the Sacred Grove. There was a Holly Month in the summer. So of course there must be a Holly elf.

"He told us what the ones in the Mall are doing to the animals. But then his reports stopped too."

"We don't know what became of them."

"Holly is a strong elf – it would take a lot to defeat him."

"Thistle isn't a pushover either! She springs up everywhere!"

"The Mall is worse than a woodworm eating a tree!"

"There are plants and flowers which are fading away without their elves to tend to them."

"Poisons come from the Mall, they're poisoning the marsh."

"And the river too."

"And it flows down to the sea."

49

How could I not have known about it? wondered Rowan. Nobody had mentioned it. We come here and meet our friends and have fun. I thought this was a world where everything was happy!

But then, she thought, in our world, there are people meeting friends and having fun, but in other places in the world, people are suffering and going through terrible things. I bet our Holly *is* there. Some lead weight in Rowan's stomach told her that's where her cousin was.

I wonder what they're doing to her right now? Is she in a kind of prison? Has she had anything to eat even?

"It is time to go to the dining hall for your dinner now," Zantia announced.

Phew, at last a break! thought Holly. But she was wrong. Zantia proceeded to lecture them on the opportunities provided by the dinner to practise their posture, polite conversation, correct way to hold cutlery and so forth, and then she asked questions to make sure they had been listening.

But at last the lecture was over, so she followed the others along a corridor and down some stairs to the dining hall. Zantia made her walk down the stairs again, more elegantly.

The hall was large, with several immaculately white tables, and people of various ages sitting at them. All around the high, white walls were photographs of models, and television screens showing advertisements of fashions. Holly saw where her class was sitting and headed for them. There were a couple of spaces, but one was next to Vectira, so she decided not to sit there, especially when Vectira remarked:

"Here's the creature - let's all watch and see what a mess she makes of sitting down!"

Holly blushed again, and pulled out a chair next to another person - was it Lucira? The chair made a scraping noise, and her classmates all snickered.

"Lift it," murmured Lucira, and Holly felt a surge of gratefulness. She lifted the chair and sat.

"Flopped like a mudball!" said Vectira, and the others snickered again sycophantically.

Holly did her best to sit straight. She wondered when the food would appear. She was very hungry and looking forward to it. They hadn't lined up to get it from a canteen like she did with school dinners, so she supposed there would be waiters to bring it. She looked for them.

There were figures in grey, with blank grey masks, carrying trays. Upon each tray were several long-stemmed glasses of water.

"Who are they?" Holly asked Lucira.

"Who?"

"Those people."

Lucira laughed a light tinkling laugh. "Oh, those aren't *people*, dear me no! Those are only attendants!"

"Oh." The blank masks and dark eyeholes were giving Holly the creeps.

"A piece of advice, dear." Lucira leant closer, and put her hand up to her perfect lips. Each fingernail was a perfect silver oval. "One never looks at them. It's considered very bad manners."

"Oh. Okay, then." It wasn't that difficult to ignore the

attendants. She didn't want to see them anyway, they were creepy. Holly lifted her glass and took a sip of water. It tasted rather odd, she was sure there was something else in it, but she wasn't sure what. Where was the food?

The first course was soup. It arrived in white dishes, a clear pink liquid, surrounded by thin white crisps arranged on the plate below. Both soup and crisps tasted salty, and slightly sweet, but didn't even begin to take the edge off Holly's appetite. All the food turned out to be the same, artistically arranged, tiny, almost tasteless, and totally inadequate. Holly's stomach began to protest. Everyone was chattering so lightly and wittily - at least, they tittered with knowing laughter, and Holly tried to join in, so as not to seem out of place. They were so beautiful and glamorous, and those they talked of very famous, "as I said to Serena," and, "as Kalibra remarked to me."

Holly was torn between desperately wanting to go home and desperately wanting to succeed.

She had to make it, she told herself. She had to.

The panel of judges looked intently at Holly.

Shoulders back, Holly told herself. Smile, sparkle! Stomach in! She felt so tense, like an elastic band stretched to the limit.

"What's your name?"

"Holly."

"Holly. Hm. Too... prickly, too *wild*. Might have to do something about that."

"Might? Certainly should, I'd say!"

"I'll change it!" piped up Holly eagerly.

52

"Hm." One judge turned to another. "Well, what do you think?"

The other judge pursed her lips with a sort of reverse-whistle. Holly's stomach clenched, filling with dread. She had to get through! She *had* to!

"We-ell, you know, I do think she *does* have some potential."

Holly's heart leapt.

"Potential? You think so? I would say the hair needs working on. And the nose."

"Oh, yes, and the fingernails. And the knees."

"And she's too fat, of course," the judges chorused, nodding their heads. Holly's stomach sank.

"But even so… Holly, how much do you want to be beautiful?"

"Ever so much!" Holly assured them.

"Ever so much?" one judge repeated in a doubtful voice.

"It's all I want! It's all I've ever wanted! I've always wanted it!" Holly told them, frantically. "Please, please, give me a chance!"

"How hard are you prepared to work?"

"Very hard! Ever so hard! I'd give a hundred per cent!" She looked at their doubting faces. One of them was tapping a pencil on the desk, held between perfectly manicured bright red fingernails. Tap tap tap.

Holly was desperate. "I'll do anything!" she assured them.

Their faces actually brightened, their red lips curved into smiles, long mascaraed eyelashes lowered over their eyes. "Excellent! That is exactly the attitude we need, Holly!"

"But you'd have to work hard."

"I will, I will!"

"And you have to really want it."

"I do, I do!"

"So, are we agreed, we give her a chance?" One judge turned to the other.

"We are agreed. Holly," the voice was almost warm, caressing, serious. "Holly, we want you to go away, and work really hard, and give a hundred percent, and then come back to us for a second interview."

Holly felt a gush of relief. "Oh, thanks! Oh, thanks ever so! I won't let you down, I promise I won't!"

The judge tilted her head on one side, turned one hand palm up. "You may go."

Holly curtseyed and left, weak with relief.

"There! Knew they'd give you a chance!" said Nexus, who was standing outside the door with another guard.

Holly's relief gave way instantly to worry. "They said I'm too fat! And my nose is wrong! My hair, my fingernails, my knees! What am I going to *do?!*"

"You'll be helped," said Nexus.

"I won't eat! I won't eat *anything!*" vowed Holly. "That way I'm *bound* to lose weight! And I've got to have something done to my hair! But what can I do about my nose? And a name! I need a new name! Something cool! Something they'll like!"

"Report to Zantia. She'll give you one. A new name for a new you!" Nexus smiled.

"Yes!" Holly's mind, fluttering like a moth, focused on the shining light of her goal – to be a model. A new her, a thinner, more glamorous her, an elegant, shining self, the kind of person everybody else is jealous of… Yes. And she wouldn't eat, and she would work so hard, and she would succeed.

"Should we be eating when Holly is missing?" wondered Rowan guiltily, looking at her stick of berry-chew.

"Think of it this way," said Linden. "We need this to build our strength up."

"That's true."

"We've walked *loads,*" pointed out Rosie, munching. "And we finished our sandwiches yesterday." They didn't become as hungry in Nuin Duir as they would in their world, but they still needed to eat.

And, as Rosie said, they had walked a lot over the past couple of days. A group of them – elves and the Three, as well as Misty – were making their way to the Mall. They had headed out of the forest, skirting round the marshes which gradually became salt marshes covered in birds, then sand and sea. Instead, they went over the hills, passing by Crone Mountain where Rowan had climbed on her Quest months ago. The hills curved downward to meadowland with long grasses and bushes, then more woodland – but in this wood, grey-black smoke could be seen rising from behind the trees. The sign of the Mall.

They slept in hammocks strung from the trees. The next morning, they turned East, to their right, leaving the wood behind. The land rose and fell, and then there was a cliff, with rocks and a beach - like the first beach they had come to in Nuin Duir, where they had met Findolf the talking dolphin, and Seashell and little Limpet and the other sea elves.

But this one was in a very different state from the beach back South. That had been fresh and clean, and full of life. There was an unpleasant smell hovering around here, and crumpled slimy scraps of cloth and plastic on the sand.

Rosie sniffed. "What is it? It smells a bit like vinegar, only…"

"Kind of chemically," agreed Rowan. "Like… nail varnish."

"Oh, look! The sea elves!" Rosie brightened.

The sea elves were sitting on some rocks. Their smooth skin was silvery white at the front and a deep blue-black on the back, and their tails were shaped like dolphins'.

Rosie waved. "Hey! Over here!"

The sea elves' sleek bald heads turned. One of them, a mother with a baby, waved her webbed fingers back.

"Seashell! Limpet!" called Rosie, and broke into a run.

Rowan followed, glad to be seeing their friends again.

But once the initial greetings were over, it became clear that all was not well.

"How's Findolf?" Rowan asked. She loved the talking dolphin, who had been her companion on her Quest, and carried her on his back.

Seashell's slanted grey-green eyes dropped, showing her long eyelashes. Her wide thin-lipped mouth became solemn. Baby Limpet clung to her and buried his face in her side.

"What?" asked Rowan. "Haven't you seen him?"

"Is he on a long journey?" asked Rosie.

Seashell exchanged uncomfortable glances with Linden and Beechen.

"What? What is it? Is Findolf all right? Where is he?" Rowan and Rosie grew increasingly alarmed.

"I've got some bad news for you," said Seashell. "Findolf is very ill."

"Ill? What sort of ill?"

"It's the pollution, you see. From the Mall. It gets worse the closer to the river you are. It spread wider than we thought it had." Seashell paused. "Findolf swam in it. He swallowed some of the water."

"But he's going to be okay?" asked Rosie, gulping. "He will be okay, won't he?"

Seashell shook her head slowly. The seashells of her bracelet clinked as she stroked Limpet's head. "He is very, very ill," she replied. "We don't think he's going to make it."

Not Findolf, thought Rowan, as they picked their way over the beach with the Three, towards the river.

"The pollution came from the river," the sea elves had told the goddesses. "Dead fish everywhere. At first some of the young ones ate them, but they threw them back up again."

"The water burns our skin."

"So we kept away. We're only on this beach because we had to show you."

"It's damaged the coral, the crabs, the rocks, everything."

They could see the damage. They could see the pollution.

A horrible slick of greyish-yellowish fluorescent stuff, was bubbling from the river, staining the beach, spreading into the waves, making everyone gasp at the stink that was sharp like vinegar, chemical like bleach, with rotten undertones.

There was a dead turtle on the beach, lying limp and yellowing. There were the skeletons of fish. There was a rotting dead seagull.

Not Findolf, thought Rowan. Don't let Findolf be like that. Don't let him be dead. Not my Findolf. Not my friend. She was cold with fear. Rosie was crying, sniffing, wiping the tears and snot away with her sleeves. But Rowan couldn't cry. She stumbled along, in a haze of shock, behind the goddesses, wondering how they could have allowed this to happen.

And wanting to see Findolf and dreading to see him.

Holly, now known as Astra, had spent the past few days working frantically. She felt exhausted and starving. And inadequate. It was Maths and they were counting calories, and the others were much better at calculating exactly how many calories were in each kind of food. Her head was spinning, and her corsets pinched her waist and ribs, making it difficult to catch her breath.

When Zantia had ordered the attendants to fit Holly with a corset and pull it tight, Holly had gasped, "Ouch!"

"One must suffer to be beautiful," Zantia had scolded. "After all, you don't *have* to be here. You could always be uncool instead. You could always be a social retard."

It was just like Chloe and Rachel at school. Holly admired them desperately and was always scared she wouldn't be cool enough to be in their gang.

She must look good… and *how* many calories were there in one of the white crisps they'd had with the soup?

After school was over, Zantia called her in to the office. "Ah, Astra. I just thought I should let you know that you owe us two hundred credits," she said in her musical voice.

"Two hundred?! But -" gasped Holly.

"Now, now, dear, please don't puff and blow so inelegantly. It would have been more, except you have done quite well on your knowledge tests. However, I thought I should let you know quite how important it is that you pass the next judge's examination. The penalty for failure is expulsion, and then the debt needs to be repaid, so you will need to work in order to do that."

Holly's heart pounded. She wanted to gasp and flounder, but her training kept her upright, hands folded in her lap. "Thank you Zantia, that was most considerate of you," she replied in a prim voice.

Zantia inclined her head and smiled approvingly with her perfect lips. "You appear before the judges tomorrow," she said.

The judges. The ones who would decide whether or not Holly – Astra – made it as a model.

She *had* to pass. Nothing else mattered.

Findolf was lying in a large rock pool, which was beyond the river, further down the beach where the water was cleaner. Sea elves were pouring water over him from large seashells, to keep him wet and comfortable. His tail moved, limply. His grey skin had reddish-black burns on it. There were sores

59

around his mouth, which gaped open, its normal cheerful smile quite gone. His eyes that usually sparkled were swollen shut.

"Oh, *Findolf!*"

Rowan and Rosie ran to him. "Findolf, wake up! It's us, Rowan and Rosie!"

One eye half opened. Findolf blew air from his blowhole, and tried to greet them, but all he could manage was a faint, "Ro…" This dolphin loved to chatter, and now he couldn't even speak.

Rowan felt as though her heart was breaking. She kept remembering Findolf laughing, playing, chattering – and how his perceptive questioning had made her admit she was being bullied at school – how, without him, that would never have been resolved with the help of the Ash Tree Goddess. He was a true friend. And now he was dying. Her throat swelled with grief, and tears stung her eyes.

Rosie turned to the Three, who were standing behind them. "You've got to *do* something!" she shouted. "You're goddesses! You've got to help him!"

"Please," added Rowan, who normally would have scolded Rosie for shouting at grown-ups. And then she burst into tears, sobbing, "Please! Please help him! *Please!* Please don't let him die!"

"What do you think?"

The judges surveyed Holly, who was holding herself tall and straight in her tight, fashionable outfit. Every fabric of her body was taut with expectation.

Danger Through The Oak by Philippa Drakeford

"We-ell. I'm sorry, Astra, it just isn't good enough."

Holly felt as though she had been punched in the stomach. She gasped. "But -! But I worked really hard!"

"Did you?" They looked at her as though she was a well-known liar coming up with yet another ridiculous story.

"Yes! I did! I did what you said! I changed my hair and my fingernails and my name and I lost weight! I've been working so hard!" Holly was frantic.

"Too bad. It's no good. You're just not of the standard we require."

"Below the standard we require."

"*Way* below it, in fact."

"Hardly beautiful. Downright plain, one might say."

"*Ugly,* in fact. And too fat, of course."

"Of course."

"You were wrong about this one," said one judge to another.

The other shook her head sorrowfully. "I know. I really believed she could do it. But she let me down. She didn't work hard enough. She just didn't *want* it enough."

"But I *did!* I *do!* Oh, please, please, give me a chance! Please, I'm begging you, I'll do anything!"

"Anything?" A raised eyebrow.

"Anything! Anything you want!"

A pause. Holly was as taut as a high-wire, her fists clenched, fingernails digging into her palms so much it hurt. Her heart was pounding. She felt dizzy and faint.

The judges were looking at each other, eyebrows raising, the corner of a mouth tilting... One of them tapped her pen, tap tap tap…

"No!" they chorused abruptly.

"But -"

"Next!"

"But -"

"Security!"

Two guards approached, and took Holly by the arm. She fainted as they dragged her away, her befuddled ears vaguely hearing the judges' purring voices.

"Ah, the next contestant… Lucira, isn't it? And how much do *you* want to be beautiful?"

CHAPTER SIX

Light poured from the Maiden's hands, soothing and sweet as milk. Her gentle face was illuminated by it, her eyes as blue-green as the sea. Everyone was silent, watching, waiting, aware of the power from her, as they felt their own auras filling with the cool energy of healing.

Rosie bit her nails. Rowan hardly dared breathe, thinking, *Oh, please! Oh, please let it be all right, please!*

Gradually, the sores on Findolf's skin began to melt away.

Oh, yes, thought Rowan, her heart lifting with hope. She could feel the healing energy, which felt like breathing out of the palms of her hands. She turned her palms towards him, and let it flow.

Findolf's body jerked. His mouth closed. His tail twitched, swished up – down - up, then slapped down energetically, sending up a splash of water right into their faces.

Gasping and wiping water from their eyes, the girls saw his own eyes opening. He sent up a puff of breath from his blowhole, followed by rapid clicks and whistles. "Hello, Rowan! Hello, Rosie!"

"Findolf!" they exclaimed.

"You soaked me, you silly thing!" Rowan half laughed and half sobbed as she flung her arms around him and hugged him.

"To be wet is good!" replied Findolf, and they all laughed.

Rowan sat back, wiping tears from her face, unable to stop smiling. His skin felt smooth and healthy once more. He smelt of the sea. Rosie was laughing, patting him, rubbing her cheek against him.

Rowan looked up at the Maiden. *"Thank you,"* she said, putting all the feelings of her heart into that one word.

The Maiden smiled, knowing all Rowan felt. "You are most welcome," she replied.

"I feel strong! I want to swim!" Findolf was declaring.

"We will call upon the sea goddess," said the Maiden.

"Thank you Maiden! Thank you, Goddess! Stand back, everybody! Big wave coming!" warned Findolf.

Rowan and Rosie and the others scrambled hastily backwards as a large blue-green wave swelled and came rushing towards them, topped with white foam. The foam was streaming backwards like white hair, or a white mane – was that a face at the top of the wave?

The wave rushed over Findolf, caught him up, and carried him back to the sea. They could hear his delighted cries.

"Findolf swims again! Swishy tail, slim fins! Findolf's strong – Findolf swims! Wha-hoo!"

Rowan and Rosie joined hands with the elves and capered around joyfully, giggling. "Findolf swims again!" they sang with happy silliness. "Swishy tail, slim fins! Findolf's strong – Findolf swims! Wha-hoo!"

They stopped dancing to watch him leap into the air… curve… and dive, sending up a fountain of water that sparkled as the sunlight hit it.

Rosie jumped up and down and clapped her hands. "Yay! Go, Findolf!"

He responded with a stream of joyful clicks and squeals. Rowan's heart sang as she watched him. This was Findolf as he should be. All was well with him now.

But all was not well with Nuin Duir.

Nobody else must suffer the way Findolf had. Nobody else must die like the seagull, the turtle, the fish. The inhabitants of the Mall must wake up to what they were doing, and stop.

"Wake up!"

Holly's head spun, she blinked. There was a guard.

"What happened?" Then she remembered. She had lost. She wasn't beautiful enough.

"You awake? Good. Come on then."

"Wh - where?" stammered Holly.

"Where losers go." The guard grinned unpleasantly.

"Wh-where's that?"

"You're about to find out!"

The guard held Holly's arm firmly and marched her away.

They stopped only to collect her old clothes so that she could change into them. Her new ones were removed by a faceless attendant. Holly's jeans still had mud on them. The guard watched scornfully as she put them on. She felt disgraced. Worse still, Vectira, Zarifa, Karina, Lucira and the others saw her through a window, stared and pointed. Holly burned with humiliation as she and the guard passed them.

Down long corridors she went, the guard always by her side, round corners, round and down until she was completely lost. At the end of the final corridor was a large steel door, with steel rivets around the edges, and a very solid looking lock.

The guard let go of her arm briefly, and undid the lock with a card, then turned a handle round and round like a steering wheel. The door creaked open, letting in light… daylight.

Holly blinked. "Outside?" She had almost forgotten that outside existed.

"Move!" ordered the guard, and outside they went. Into huge multi-coloured piles of something… of cloth, wet cloth, with puddles and stains, and bits of rotting food… and the air was choked with unpleasant smells.

"What's all this?" asked Holly.

"Rubbish. Clothes," replied the guard.

"You mean you just throw everything away? All those clothes?" gasped Holly.

"Of course. They're yesterday's," said the guard.

"But it's such a waste!" It was a novel thought for Holly. Suddenly faced with the reality of those huge heaps of rejected things, she couldn't help but be appalled.

"We have to keep up with fashion. It keeps the economy going."

Then Holly saw something really horrible. It was a thin white hand, each finger tipped with a bright red fingernail… it was on a thin white arm… which was connected to a thin, pale body, and there was a thin, pale hollow-cheeked face with its eyes closed.

Her heart thumped and she felt sick. "That's – that's not a *body*, is it?" she whispered. "That person looks *dead.*"

"Oh yeah, she's dead all right," said the guard indifferently.

"But – don't you bury dead people or anything? She's just lying there! Like a piece of rubbish!"

"Dead bodies are rubbish. Death's ugly. Bodies are useless. Why should we care what happens to them? They just go down the chute like everything else."

"But it's all just lying here in heaps, making the air all smelly and horrible!"

The guard shrugged again. "So what? We live in the Mall, our air's all air-conditioned. Only the grubs and criminals have to breathe this air, and who cares what they breathe? It's not like they matter."

Holly was so horrified that she couldn't speak at all for a moment. "I wonder who she was?" she whispered.

"Oh, she was one of the models, you can tell, she's so thin. You see, they have to starve themselves to be thin enough to fit into the clothes, and nobody can live for long without eating. So they die."

"And nobody *does* anything?"

"Why should they? The models don't live long, that's true, but while they're alive, they're the most admired, the most glorious, the coolest and most fashionable. And if you'd rather be uncool than dead, well!" The guard snickered scornfully.

Holly felt sick as they approached a grey concrete building.

As soon as the guard opened the door, Holly was hit by the noise, the clatter and thump of hundreds of machines. The damp, warmish, stuffy air hit her lungs, it was like breathing through an old sock. They were in a large room with a low ceiling and harsh lights, and there were hundreds of elves in there. They wore grey. Unlike the uniformly silver-white Malltonians, these people were various colours, brown, golden, pink – but all of them had an unhealthy greyish yellow tint to their skin and dark greyish purple circles under their eyes. They were hunched over machines, stitching or cutting, they were carrying boxes and bundles of cloth, and some were sweeping the floor. All of them looked exhausted and miserable. Guards strode around, watching.

One guard marched over. "No experience?" he questioned.

"No," admitted Holly.

"Right, we'll start you as a cutter-snatcher."

He led her to a big machine. Cloth was fed into it, and every now and again, a huge shiny razor-sharp blade would whip downwards with a thunk and slice the cloth into a particular shape – Holly recognised it as part of a pattern that made up a jacket. The shape was then picked up by a sort of metal finger that used suction, and then spat onto a conveyor belt that led away, first to inspectors, and then to join other pieces, and then to the stitchers.

Holly's job was to snatch the piece of cloth that was left once the pattern had been cut, then pass it on. "And do it quick," grinned the guard. "That blade's very sharp. Here! Grub! Show her your hand!" He grabbed a hunched figure who was sweeping the floor. Holly had a glimpse of a pale wrinkled face and unhappy eyes, and then gasped. The guard held the sweeper's arm in one fist and shoved it under Holly's nose. There were only two fingers left on her hand.

"This grub wasn't quick enough," sniggered the guard. "Now you'll be quick, won't you? Unless you want to end up like Stumpy here! Come on, chop chop!" He laughed aloud at his joke, cuffed the sweeper round the head, and she whimpered and scuttled away. Holly gulped.

"There is poison in the water."

"The fish have died."

"The reeds are yellowing. Look at them." The elf Reed held out her hand, towards them, her own skin a sickly yellow to match the plants she looked after.

"The insects and worms are poisoned and die. The birds and fish who eat the them become ill and die."

The Three watched and listened, and nodded. The goddess of the River, who appeared to be made of water, and thus was fascinatingly transparent, was telling the Three of what was happening. The elves of the plants of the river and marshes were giving their reports too.

Rowan and Rosie were sitting on a fallen tree, a little way

back, watching the polluted river flowing past, and the group of sorrowful elves surrounding the Three. One brought a sickly wading bird to the Maiden, who laid her hand upon its head, and healed it.

"Why didn't the Three come before?" asked Rowan. "Why did they let this happen?"

"The Goddess is wild, you know, she comes when she does," replied Beechen. "She manifests in many ways, sometimes as the Three."

"It's free will, freedom to choose," explained Linden. "We are not puppets. They don't interfere."

"So why are they here now then?" asked Rowan. "If they don't interfere? The Maiden healed that bird -"

"And Findolf, and I'm glad she did!" interrupted Rosie.

"Me too!" agreed Rowan. "But I don't understand. Healing is interfering, surely. But why Findolf and not… well, there was a dead turtle on the beach. And a dead seagull. Why him and not them? It doesn't seem fair."

"The Three can't go round healing every single little illness," said Linden. "They would never stop! Besides, illness is a sign that something is wrong. You have to put the wrong right. If there were no signs, how would you know things were imbalanced? It's like pain. If there wasn't any pain…"

"You could stick your hand in a fire and not know it's burnt," agreed Rowan. "I've heard of a disease called leprosy where people don't feel any pain, and they can damage themselves easily without noticing it. I understand They can't heal *everything*. But why now? That's what I don't understand."

70

"Hang on a moment, we need to hear this." Beechen held up one hand. "The River goddess is explaining more about what happens inside the Mall."

They got up and hurried forward.

"… from Holly's last report," the River goddess was saying. She passed one hand through her hair, which was green and flattish like water weeds. "There is a Boss in charge of the Mall. It is he who began all the damage. But many others go along with it. They care only for clothes, and their own appearance. The manufacture of those clothes, and the paint for their faces and the substances to style their hair – those processes pollute my river. But also they burn trees for energy…"

"Care only for clothes? Holly should fit right in!" remarked Rosie.

"Sh!" Rowan put a finger to her lips. "I'm listening."

"But there are those inside the Mall who see the wrongness of this. Holly was trying to encourage them, he said. He was struggling, because the people there do not eat properly, they do not think clearly. He said he was getting through to some of them. There are guards, though, who would want to put him in prison. I haven't seen him since. Nobody has. We don't know what became of him, or Thistle, who went before him."

There were mutters of agreement and concern from the assorted elves. "They are not the only ones. Many other elves have vanished into the Mall, elves of meadow and marsh and pond. We haven't seen some of them for several summers."

71

The Mother rose to speak, and everyone fell silent. "Choices were made. But there is a limit, and that limit has been passed, and enough of you have asked for our help." Her brown eyes met Rowan's, and Rowan understood that asking for help was essential. The Mother's next words confirmed it. "So we came." She turned to the River goddess and the elves. "Sisters, brothers, we hear your pain. The time has come. We shall head upriver. We shall go to the Mall together. We shall do what has to be done."

Holly was exhausted, her head spinning from the sounds of the machines, her arms and hands aching from the constant snatching of cloth she had to do. And the fear was the worst thing – the constant terror that if she was a split-second too late, the blade would chop her fingers off. Just the thought of that made her feel sick. She knew she was beginning to whimper, her hands were beginning to shake, she knew she couldn't take much more of this. How could people keep this up for hours on end?

She thought she might have been able to cope if it wasn't for the guards, who kept urging her, "Faster! Faster! You'll never meet your targets if you dawdle like that! Come on, you lazy grub!"

Eventually, she had turned around and screamed at them: "I'm doing it as fast as I can! I never worked so hard in my life before and you keep having a go at me!"

The guard had promptly slapped her face. "Shut up! You've just lost your dinner break for being insubordinate!"

Holly had put one hand to her stinging face, aghast. She

had never been hit before in her life. "How can you treat people like this?" she demanded.

"Clothes have to be made quickly to keep up with the demands of fashion, and they have to be made cheaply. Cheaper is better. More profit. In today's competitive world, we have to cut costs. Now get moving!"

"And remember, every spoiled piece of cloth is deducted from your credits!" added the other guard.

One of the other workers had kindly pulled out some of the pieces while this was going on. She nodded to Holly, who nodded back, pressing her lips together so as not to cry. She started work again. She had no choice. The machines were switched off for ten minutes, giving the others a break to eat their food in, but Holly was ordered to sweep up. The food was a kind of dry biscuit, and there was some kind of a drink too – unappetising, but Holly's mouth was dry and her stomach empty. She longed for anything.

Then, all too soon, the machines were switched on, and the terrifying desperate routine began again.

Oh no, here came the guards again! They marched right up to Holly, and she hunched her shoulders, ready to ignore the taunts and orders.

Instead, one of them announced. "You - come with us. There's been a mistake."

"A mistake?" asked Holly, faintly, staring.

"Come with us," repeated the guard.

"What're you staring at, you grubs? Get on with your work!" snapped the other, who was taller than the first.

Holly's mind was whirling as she was marched away, out of

the horrible factory, through corridors, and through a big door. "What's happening?" she asked. "Where are you taking me?"

"The Boss wants to see you," replied the taller guard. He sounded awed.

"You've got to look presentable first," said the shorter one.

They took her to a bathroom, all tiled in pristine sparkling white, with a toilet, basin and shower-bath in it. There was a large fluffy towel warming on a heated towel rail of what looked like gold. The taps were the same, even the handle of the toilet was gold. Holly would have been impressed with the luxury, but she couldn't forget the factory floor and those poor people.

"You can wash here, Astra," said the shorter guard.

Holly didn't want that name any more. "I'm called Holly, actually," she said.

"Holly?" He blinked, frowning slightly. "That reminds me of… something…" He paused, then shook his head. "No. I don't remember. I'm called Yarris. Go on, get washed. I'm sure you need it." He sounded almost kind. "The attendant will help you."

The grey-robed attendant stepped forward.

"We'll wait outside for you," said Yarris. He and the other guard left, and the attendant helped Holly take off her dirty clothes.

The other workers would still be hungry, thirsty, exhausted, in amongst clattering machines…Still, it was very nice to have a warm shower with the scented shower gel, and be clean again. Holly had always hated being dirty. Unlike her cousins, she thought. She wondered what they were doing now. She'd hardly thought of them at all. There was a special padded seat in an egg shaped alcove, which blew hot air onto her hair to dry it afterwards, and the attendant brushed it for her.

The attendant gave her new clothes: a short skirt, and a shirt with padded shoulders and a lacy collar, and slip-on shoes with small heels. All were shocking pink. Holly put them on. Then the attendant hung a pendant around her neck, a heart-shaped pink one.

Was she being given another chance? Perhaps the judges had relented? Perhaps she could be a model after all? She imagined the expression on Vectira's face, she and the others when she told them, and when they saw her being a model. They would be gutted! That would be fantastic.

"Please go to the door," said the attendant.

Holly obeyed. The door opened and the two guards looked at her approvingly. "That's better. The Boss will be happier with that," said Yarris.

"Who's the Boss? Why do they want to see me? Is it a he or a she?" asked Holly.

The guards looked uncomfortable.

"The Boss is the Boss! He's the leader of us all, he's responsible for all of us," replied Yarris. "There was a mistake, you see."

"I wouldn't want to be in the shoes of whoever is responsible!" The other guard shook his head and smirked a bit, as if the thought of someone else being punished pleased him. "You should never have been sent down."

Holly felt an enormous relief. "But why does he want to see me?"

"You'll see."

CHAPTER SEVEN

Holly's footsteps were loud on the shiny black floor. The Boss's office was large, and one wall was covered in screens showing images from CCTV cameras, the latest adverts and graphs of profits. There, behind a huge dark grey desk, was a man. To Holly's surprise, he wasn't an elf like the other people - he was human, dressed in a dark grey suit, crisp white shirt and tie. He had short blond hair, and he grinned at her with teeth that were white and perfect. "Aha! Holly, isn't it? Come in, I do apologise for the way you've been treated - it was a mistake, should never have happened."

"It's not just me," said Holly, "What about all the others in that factory?"

"Oh, that's all right, they're used to it, really. They're not like you and me. Besides, it's not your concern, it's just part of the system," he said smoothly, "It's *you* I'm interested in. If I had seen the CCTV pictures sooner, I would have had you brought to me straight away. You see," he looked at her.

"You're human. From my world."

"Yeah," said Holly, wondering what that had to do with it.

"I need a fellow human. These elves don't understand enough, really. We humans have the drive, the entrepreneurial spirit, the ambition to make a go of the system! I knew as soon as I saw you that you were that sort of girl!"

Holly felt flattered. "Well…"

"Oh, come now, don't be modest! You've got a business mind, I know it! And you know the importance of looking your best, don't you. Of fashion!"

"Well, yeah, I do."

"Better than other people. I bet some people don't understand. They don't make the effort to look good - those kind of people really irritate me!"

"Oh, me too!" gushed Holly eagerly, encouraged by his flattery. "Like my cousins - they have like, no sense of fashion at all! Knitted jumpers! Pur-lease! Like - hello? - it's the twenty-first century!"

"Excellent! Just what I need! You see, at some point I will want to retire. I've got a nice little set-up here, but I won't be doing this the rest of my life. I need someone to take over - a second in command for now - an executive. How would you like to be an executive, Holly?"

"An executive!" Holly's eyes shone. *That* would show her cousins! And everybody! For a moment she imagined saying, "I'm too *busy* to see you right now, Mummy!" She felt a spurt of glee. That would serve her right for dumping her on some smelly farm in the country!

"You would have your own office, your own desk, the latest technology, plenty of assistants working for you to bring your fashion ideas to fruition. You would have the best clothes, the best meals, the best leisure time. You would have to work hard, of course, but I'm sure you're not afraid of hard work. After all, you put a lot of work into your appearance, don't you?"

"Oh yes," agreed Holly. "I'm always reading the latest magazines for fashion tips! And you have to watch what you eat and what you wear - don't want to drop behind!"

"Exactly! Excellent - you have an excellent mind!" He grinned at her again, and she felt pleased. "Now all you have to do is learn the system."

"The system? You have to keep up with fashion to gain credits, and-"

"No, the real system. What's behind it all. What's really going on."

Holly started to feel uncomfortable. She had been thinking the Boss was a very pleasant person, obviously he had good taste, and he liked her. But now she remembered the factory, and the rubbish dump again. Were the elves different enough not to mind that kind of work? Did he know about the rubbish dump? He was grown up, so perhaps he did know best. But if he'd seen it, worked there like she had...

"Tell me, Holly, how do you get people to buy fashion products?"

"Advertise," replied Holly promptly.

"And what do you say in the adverts?"

"Tell them it's a good product? That they'd like it?"

"But just suppose they say, 'Well, I'm happy with what I have. I don't need your product!' What then?"

"Er…"

He sprang to his feet and began to pace. "You have to do more than say it's good! You have to hook them, haul them in! And in order to do that, what do you do? I'll tell you." He fixed her with a piercing gaze. "This is the secret! This is the big one! Are you listening?"

Holly nodded.

His voice sank low, conspiratorially. *"You have to make them feel bad about themselves!"*

Holly blinked. That was it? The big secret? "But surely adverts are about making people feel *good* about themselves! I mean, people are happy in adverts, happy wearing the latest clothes and make-up and things. The models are always smiling…"

The Boss shook his head. "Ah, now you're disappointing me, Holly. Think about it! Don't you see?"

Holly's heart thumped. She didn't want to disappoint him. She thought. "They're happy in the adverts," she said slowly, "because they're using the product."

"Yes! That's my girl! They're only happy because they're using the product! The adverts make them feel that without the product, they won't be cool and won't be happy! That they'll be uncool! Fat! Ugly! Outcast! Losers!"

Holly remembered the body on the rubbish tip. Suddenly, this didn't seem like a good idea.

But the Boss was in full flow now. "Contented customers don't buy products! And we want them to buy! More and more! Markets have to expand, we must have growth! It's no good just saying our products are good. You have to make the customer feel dissatisfied. And if you want them to keep on buying - which we do, I mean, it's no good a customer buying one shirt that lasts five years, it's much more profitable if they want one every six months - then you have to make them dissatisfied *all the time!*"

"That's why fashion keeps changing," said Holly slowly.

"Exactly! You have a business brain, my dear! And the best business to be in is the body business - fashion, make-up and food! People always have their bodies. They are always there. There are so many opportunities to make them feel bad about their bodies - if not their hair, then their legs, their waist, their bottom, their teeth, their feet, their hands, their nose, their eyes! You tell them this is the right way to make up your eyes, then when they get that right, you move onto their lips, or teeth, then you change to the legs, you go through all of their body - but by the time they've got it all in fashion, you change the eyes again!" He chortled and rubbed his hands. "It's like painting the Forth Bridge - it never stops! And of course the models in the photos are touched up by computer. Nobody can be that perfect."

Holly's stomach was churning.

"The other marvellous thing is that it's the fashion to be thin. I don't know who first thought that one up in our world - thin women - but whoever he was, he was a genius! Do you know why?"

"Why?"

"Because women aren't *supposed* to be thin! They're

81

supposed to have curves, to have some body fat. They need it to store their hormones in, to keep the chemical balance of their bodies. Now, all we have to do is tell them they're too fat, and what do they do? They stop eating enough food. And that means they're not getting enough nutrients to their brain. It makes them weak, easily led, more likely to be obsessive about food and fashion."

"It's not just women who follow fashion, though," said Holly.

"No, that's a matter of expanding markets. The industry in the world you and I come from had reached pretty much every woman in the West. But markets have to expand! Where else to go?"

"Other countries?"

"Well yes, the West is exporting body hatred. Take Fiji. Bulimia used to be unknown - you know what bulimia is?"

"Eating food and then vomiting it up after."

"Exactly! Well, MTV arrived in Fiji - lots of images of ultra thin models - and within a few years, one in ten teenage girls was throwing up her food! Sure customers! Hooked! And you have Chinese and Japanese women having plastic surgery to make their eyes look more Western. Of course, plastic surgery is an expanding market. If I had the qualifications, I could have gone in for it myself... But the other way to expand the market is down the age group, so they targeted girls - teenagers, then pre-teens. The Gurleez dolls for example, teaching primary school girls to be obsessive about their bodies - you have the dolls, the cartoons, the magazine, the clothes. Now they're moving out to target men and boys - and it's working. In the old days, boys used to go out and get all grubby, covered in mud playing football and climbing trees and so on. Nowadays they won't - they don't want to get their designer clothes messy! And of course, they're taking less exercise, so they'll put on weight - more customers for the diet industry!"

"If all that's happening in our world, why did you come here?" asked Holly.

He pulled a face. "Too much competition! The market's practically full, the big corporations know what they're doing. The first time I got here was by accident, but I saw right away here was a whole new world - a whole new opportunity to build my own business empire! All those customers! Of course, it wasn't easy at first. They were living in the woods and fields, getting everything they needed from there. They were distressingly happy! Like pigs in mud!"

"How did you make them unhappy?"

"Oh, a bit here, a bit there, drip drip. They were naturally very curious, so I brought them technology, all kinds of gadgets, and I brought them sweets too, and they wanted to try them out, so they passed them round and told their friends. Everyone wanted to see the things I had." He smiled. "Now, part of it was very clever, even if I say so myself. I got them hooked on sugar. Did you know sugar is addictive?"

"No." Holly knew, vaguely that sugar was supposed to be "bad for you," but not much else.

"It is, you know. Of course, a little bit of sugar won't do you any harm, provided you have a reasonably healthy nutritious diet. But if you don't…" He rubbed his hands.

"They tried some, they wanted more, they couldn't get enough. And it ruined their appetites, so they weren't eating proper nutritious food. That meant their brains weren't working properly, so their minds were more susceptible to my suggestions. They couldn't think easily. And of course, it began to affect their weight, so then I could make them feel bad about that, introduce the concept of diets. Hungry, exhausted, their blood sugar going up and down like a yo-yo – people like that are very easy to manipulate."

"I see," said Holly.

"I introduced the concept of money. They wanted more sweets and more gadgets, but I told them nothing was free, they had to pay for them. Started to build the Mall. Got them to feel the earth was dirty, the rain annoying, that they needed shelter. They lapped it up, moved in to the Mall. I used flattery and criticism to get them obsessed with clothes - and computer images of how perfect they could look. Catch 'em young, that's the thing. Once they were reliant on the Mall, reliant on me to feed them, I made sure they were never getting quite enough - addled their brains! Fed them constant adverts - it became easy!"

He stood in front of her, beaming. "Clever, eh?"

"Very," replied Holly.

"So now you see how clever and profitable it all is, you'll want to join me! Come on then, Holly! What do you say?"

CHAPTER EIGHT

"Oh, *no.*" Rowan shook her head slowly from side to side, appalled.

"The poor trees," mourned Linden. "This was woodland once."

"And meadow, and marsh with ponds," agreed Beechen. "Full of flowers, and birds, squirrels, frogs, insects, all kinds of life."

"All gone." Misty tucked her head under Rosie's chin.

"It's the horrible-ist thing I've ever seen," said Rosie, her jaw jutting with anger. "How could they?"

They had finally reached the Mall. There it was, the source of all the pollution, a vast grey concrete and metal dome, and all around it was wasteland: heaps of rotting rubbish, paper, cloth, plastic, grey ashes, and bones. Here and there, the stumps of trees poked through, like teeth in a corpse's jawbone. Dirty yellow-grey smoke rose from the Mall's stubby chimneys; and harsh chemicals and dyes – sickly pinks, acid greens, sulphur yellows – gushed and bubbled from pipes in the wall, to sink into the soil or pour into the river.

Rowan turned to the Three, who were standing silent, with solemn eyes, surveying the ruin of this part of Nuin Duir.

"You are going to do something, aren't you?" she asked.

"Indeed we are," replied the Mother regally. "Those in the Mall have wronged the land and the many beings and the Web of Life. They must be stopped."

"The land must be healed again," agreed the Maiden, her normally merry freckled face full of sorrow. "The trees and plants must grow again, and the wildlife return to the land."

"But the trees can't grow with all this rubbish, all these chemicals," said Linden. "They would be poisoned by it. The seeds won't germinate."

"It's so *big,*" said Rowan. "How can we stop it? How can we even get in to rescue Holly let alone stop the whole Mall? All the people in there… The people in charge. The guards. They'll try and stop us. What can we do?"

"Can we fight them?" asked Rosie. Her eyes gleamed. "It'd be brilliant! We could get stones and throw them at 'em, and get sticks and hit 'em, and -"

"Have you ever been in a real fight, Rosie?" asked the Mother.

"Well, no…" admitted Rosie. "I've seen them on the telly,"

"You would not enjoy a real fight. People get hurt," said the Mother.

"Blood and bruises, broken bones, and sometimes death," added the Crone. "There is nothing glorious about violence, though many stories are told to charm people into committing it."

"Besides," said the Mother, "if a friend of yours wasn't eating properly and cared only for clothes, would you hit her? Or would you try and reason with her, and help her?"

"Well, help her," admitted Rosie.

"Reason with her," agreed Rowan, "But it's not just not eating properly, it's pollution! It's hurting people, and animals and the land!" She was wringing her hands, quivering with distress.

"I know, my dear, we feel it too," said the Maiden sympathetically. "All that pain."

"So what can we do?" asked Rowan. "What can we *do?*"

Yarris was waiting for Holly after the Boss had finished seeing her, along with an attendant.

"You'll be wanting to change your clothes for dinner," said Yarris.

"Mm." Holly wasn't really listening.

"Let me take your pendant," offered the attendant, reaching out.

"I want to wear it to dinner," said Holly, putting a hand over it.

"No!" exclaimed Yarris. The attendant's head turned sharply towards him.

"What's the matter?" asked Holly.

"We must have it!" Yarris sounded so agitated that Holly

became very curious.

"Sh!" the attendant hissed at him.

Holly closed her hand round the pendant and held it tightly. "I won't give it to you till you tell me. Why do you want it so much?"

"It's not yours, it's just on loan so you could look your best when you see the Boss," said Yarris smoothly, but Holly didn't believe him.

"The truth," she said.

"Are you for the Boss?" asked the attendant.

Holly hesitated. This could be a trick. She couldn't tell what the attendant was thinking, or feeling, or anything about them – even if they were male or female. If she said no, they could throw her back to the factory again. She looked into Yarris's eyes. They were very dark green. Could she trust him? But it was time to tell the truth, now she knew what the Boss did. "No," she admitted. "I told him I needed time to think. But that was just to put him off."

They looked at each other. "Dangerous," said Yarris.

"But what she's heard and seen," said the other.

"It's a transmitter," said Yarris finally. "We wanted to know the Boss's secrets, what he said to you. It's been recording it."

Holly nodded, then took off the necklace and handed it to Yarris. "Thanks," he said.

"Come with us," invited the attendant. The grey-robed figure moved down the corridor, to a discreet door in the side that Holly hadn't noticed before, slid it aside and went through.

Holly and Yarris followed.

Once inside, the attendant pulled off her hooded mask to reveal a light brown face, green eyes and purple hair that stuck up in fluffy spikes. She looked tired, but very alive, and determined. "These are the attendants' corridors," she explained. "So that we may appear and serve the Malltonians as inconspicuously as possible."

"What's your name?" asked Holly. Somehow it seemed important to know.

"I was called Nubitha when I was at fashion school."

"You were at fashion school? Like me?"

"Oh yes." Nubitha ran one hand through her purple hair. "I wanted to become a model at first, and perfect. But it was so much effort – especially trying to make my hair conform. And everybody was so cruel to each other and to me, and I found myself becoming cruel too. It just all seemed so pointless. I wanted to find a different way – surely there had to be something else, I thought. But I didn't know what it would be. My marks fell, my appearance did too. I ended up in the factory. But I did well there, and they promoted me to be an attendant."

"That's a promotion? Being invisible, serving everybody?"

Nubitha smiled and her green eyes gleamed. "There are advantages to being invisible. And attendants have more time to think than factory workers do. Forbidden thoughts. Like rebellion."

"Come on, let's get moving," urged Yarris.

"You'll have to take your shoes off first. Too noisy," said Nubitha, reaching into her robe and handing Holly a pair of soft black canvas shoes with thick felt soles.

No wonder attendants could move so silently, thought Holly, as she put them on. Carrying her other shoes, which had clopped loudly when she walked, Holly padded noiselessly after the others.

Chapter Nine

Holly felt excited and scared at the same time. She hadn't realised that there were rebels here in the Mall, both attendants and guards. She had just met some of them, a group of about ten. They weren't the only ones either, they had told her. They had shared food – dried berries and nuts, and her stomach stopped complaining.

And now that Holly knew exactly what they were fighting, she felt a clear, vigorous energy. She wanted to be a part of this fight. It was a fight against injustice, a fight that must be won. She was ashamed of how muzzy-minded she had been, how easily she had fallen into thinking that only looks and winning prizes mattered. No more. Her mind was clear.

She was walking with the others now, trying to be inconspicuous. And it was quite easy. Concealed beneath the grey robes of an attendant, everybody ignored her. She passed some of the girls from her class, Vectira, Zarifa, Karina and Lucira who were comparing the points they'd got for make-up, deportment, appearance and so on. Holly couldn't resist sticking her tongue out at them. The fact that they had no idea gave her immense satisfaction.

The rebels had a plan.

In the secret attendants' room, Yarris and Nubitha had introduced Holly to the others. They had wiped their silver make-up off their faces, revealing skins in various shades of brown. Yarris had very dark brown skin to go with his dark green eyes, and short dark green spiky hair under his helmet. Holly had thought how much better they looked with their natural colouring. Eagerly, they had crowded round the pendant, talking in whispers – had it worked?

Yarris had unflipped the heart of the pendant and removed something, fitting it into a socket on the computer. On the screen was a rather blurred image of the Boss. He was speaking. They listened for some time.

"This is *dynamite!*" Yarris had whispered excitedly.

"What'll you do with it?" asked Holly.

"Broadcast it to everyone, over the screens, along with the other material we've been collecting. Once they hear and see this, the Boss will be overthrown, and we'll be free!"

That was the plan.

Smooth smarmy voices from elves with silver faces and

gleaming white smiles proclaimed their messages from every huge screen in the Mall Square.

"Have YOU got the latest fashions yet? Don't get left behind!"

"Serena has the most up-to-date outfits ever! Do YOU?"

"Want the latest fashions, but behind with your credit? We give you up to ONE THOUSAND CREDITS with our NEW SUPER PLATINUM credit card! A high credit limit so you can SPEND SPEND SPEND! And it's so easy! Simply click on the link to enter FASHION HEAVEN!" Small text ran rapidly across the foot of the screen to say that all the money must be paid back, with compound interest, within the limited time, or the debtor would be subject to arrest, but it was virtually unreadable.

"Oh, look, it's *Kalibra!* She's my *favourite!*" twittered Lucira, clutching at Zarifa's arm. The elves from Holly's class were in the Square, on a homework assignment.

On screen, the model Kalibra was swaying on top of incredibly high heels, her stick-thin legs encased in skin-tight leggings to emphasise their thinness. Her wasp-waisted jacket was trimmed with fluffy fur. She was smiling brightly, fluttering long mascaraed eyelashes. She sang: "I've got the latest! Now I look chic! I must stay thin! Don't want to look a freak!"

A deep voice proclaimed: "STAY CHIC like Kalibra, with our newest, best fashions yet!"

"She's so beautiful! She's my thinspiration! Do you think I'm beginning to look like her? Just a little bit?" wondered Lucira, wistfully.

"Well, you're too *fat* of course," began Vectira, with a tinkling laugh, making Karina titter and raise one perfectly manicured set of fingernails to her lips, as though she were showing them off rather than just covering her mouth.

And then Vectira and Karina's laughter died away into gurgles of surprise.

"THIS IS THE PRICE OF THE CLOTHES YOU WEAR," announced a deep voice, as all the screens turned black.

The fur-trimmed jacket that Kalibra had been modelling appeared, then faded. Behind it were rows upon rows of cramped cages with small furry animals in them, some whimpering and clawing and biting the bars, other hunched and silent, miserable suffering lumps of fur. The cages were as filthy as the room.

There were shocked gasps.

Holly, in her attendant's uniform, caught Nubitha's eye in hers. Nubitha gave a quick nod.

Then the factory appeared on the screen, the rows of machines, the workers. A voice told everyone what long hours they worked. There was a photograph of the sweeper that the guard had called 'Stumpy' – showing her hand with only two fingers.

Crowds were gathering. There were shocked whispers and murmurs.

"I don't get it," Karina was saying, in a puzzled voice "This is an awfully strange advertising campaign. Is it meant to be ironic?"

"No, it's *real*, you idiot!" said Lucira, sharply. "It's real."

She blinked, eyes on the screens, and shook her head. "It was like this all the time, and we never thought... never stopped it..."

Oh yes! thought Holly, jubilantly. It's working! It is!

And then came the big announcement. "You are about to hear the voice of the Boss speaking. This tells you all exactly what he thinks of you."

Over footage of the rubbish dumps and the dead bodies, the factory and the fur, the Boss spoke of his planning and scheming. *"You have to make them feel bad about themselves!"*

"I can't get my head round this! I feel quite faint!" Karina put one hand to her forehead, as the Boss explained how sugar addiction, poor nutrition and low blood sugar kept the elves brainless and biddable.

"We should do something!" declared Lucira.

"This isn't *really* the Boss," Vectira's voice rose, shrill with indignation. "He wouldn't do that! It's a trick — someone's trying to trick us!"

"Yes, that's what it is!" agreed Karina. "It must be!"

"No it isn't!" protested Lucira.

There were similar arguments all around the crowd. Nubitha, Holly and the other rebels darted quick-footed from one group of elves to the next, putting in comments such as, "He's tricked us for years!" and, "We must do something! We must rebel against the Boss! We must release the prisoners!" Holly was growing more and more excited. It was working!

But at that moment, the screens flickered and went black again. Then a guard appeared on screen. Holly recognised

Nexus. He looked grim. Two guards behind him held a struggling elf that Holly recognised from the rebel group. Her name was Zest. "This is an urgent announcement. A ridiculous hoax has been played on you all by a group of stupid, lying, dangerous rebels," began Nexus.

"There! I *told* you so!" proclaimed Vectira.

"Oh yes, I knew all along!" chipped in Karina, eagerly.

"Hush!" Zantia put one finger to her lips.

"But -" began Lucira, frowning.

"They were jealous of our Boss, to whom we owe so much. They were jealous because they weren't beautiful enough to be models – as you can see from the wretched example our guards have caught." Nexus smirked, waving one hand towards Zest.

"Don't believe him! The Boss is tricking us! Set us free," Zest began to shout, then one of the guards clapped a hand over her mouth.

"See? Hysterical, quite hysterical. So the best thing for you all to do is to return to your homes while we round up the rebels. This little matter can be sorted out quite easily. There are guards appearing to help escort you to your homes now. I repeat, return to your homes. We will open the shops earlier tomorrow to make up for lost shopping time today."

"Don't believe him!" Lucira began to shout. "The films were real!"

"Don't be silly!" said Vectira.

Two guards appeared as if from nowhere, and grabbed Lucira's arms. "We have reason to believe you're in league with the rebels," said one.

96

"What? No! I never knew till I saw -" began Lucira.

"Come with us." They marched away, with Lucira in between them, tottering on her fashionable shoes and looking dazed.

"There! I always knew there was something funny about her!" proclaimed Vectira.

"Well, she never quite made the grade when it came to looks, did she?" put in Karina. "Jealousy, you see, just like Nexus said!"

Holly didn't stay for the rest of the conversation. Her heart was pounding. There were guards everywhere. She tried to hurry away, but everywhere she went there were guards, marching in between the rapidly dwindling crowd of elves, questioning, arresting. They were even breaking tradition by unmasking the attendants, and dragging them off. Where was Nubitha?

"Holly!"

Holly's head whipped round towards the hissed voice. Nubitha was lurking near the entrance of a building, beckoning rapidly. "This way!"

Holly walked as rapidly as she could, then heard a guard shout, "There! That attendant – the clumsy-looking one! Get it!" and broke into a run.

As Holly and Nubitha wound their way between displays of clothes, Holly gasped, "They caught Zest – did they get Yarris too?"

"I don't know yet," replied Nubitha in a tight voice. "They were both responsible for putting the films on. This way."

Quickly, in through a plain door which led to the

attendants' corridors, out of the lights and noise into plain dimness – but there were multiple footsteps, echoing throughout the tunnels as attendants and rebels alike fled.

"Nubitha! Holly!" It was Yarris, his face a mask of distress. "They caught us! We were staying to make sure the broadcast went all right! They grabbed us both, we struggled – I got away but Zest didn't! What are we going to do? It's all gone wrong!"

"I don't know! They're arresting us all over the place!" replied Nubitha. "And it was nearly working!"

"Was it?" Yarris's dark green eyes lit with hope.

"Yeah," confirmed Holly. "People were saying we should do something. Some people. Others didn't believe it… but some did!"

"Then the idea is out there! It won't die – even if we do!"

"Down here! Fetch out the rebels!"

They froze at the harsh shout of a guard, then, without even looking at each other, set off running down the corridors.

"Yuck!" Rosie lifted one foot and flicked it, so that the slimy piece of cloth flew off the end. "Things keep *crunching* under my feet."

"Mine too." Rowan grimaced. "I'm glad we're wearing boots." She paused. Her eye had caught something… something long and thin and pale… was that a mannequin's arm? No. With a chill, she realised it was a real arm, a real hand which was tipped with bright red fingernails - a dead body.

Rosie mustn't see it!

Quickly, Rowan turned to the elves, as a distraction. "Are you okay, Linden, Beechen? It isn't very nice to walk on, is it?"

The elves, who had bare feet, were looking very uncomfortable. Linden shook her head. "I don't like it. It is harsh. I can't feel the earth singing."

"I feel foot-blind," agreed Beechen. "It's horrible."

They were all clambering on the rubbish heap, close to the Mall, bringing armfuls of rotten wood to the Crone, who was standing beside her cauldron, waiting, a tall, impressive figure in black.

"This one has a maggot in it," reported Rosie, holding out part of a branch. "I can see it wriggling."

"Excellent." The Crone inclined her head. "And I see that a couple of yours have fungus growing on them, Rowan."

"Yes, Lady," agreed Rowan, who wanted to call the Crone something polite but thought that 'Ma'am' didn't sound right somehow. "The end crumbled away when I picked it up. This bit's kind of spongy."

"Just what I need."

"I have a toadstool, and a mushroom," said Linden.

"I have worms," Beechen offered his handful of squirming earthworms.

"I found a beetle!" squeaked Misty, who was on Rosie's shoulder, her whiskers quivering. "It's tickle tickle tickle on my paws, wriggly wriggly wriggly legs!"

"Good. Throw them in the cauldron, then. All of you."

They threw their loads into the black iron cauldron that

was exactly like a witch's cauldron in a book, then rubbed the bits from the palms of their hands, and brushed down their jumpers and tunics – or, in Misty's case, her fur.

The Crone began to chant. Strange words that made the goose pimples rise on the girls' arms, and prickled the backs of their necks. They could feel a powerful swirling energy, a deep vibration. The Crone raised her arms, her head tilted back, a deep sound emanated from her open her mouth...

Then, in one swift move, she lifted the cauldron, and emptied the brown mixture over the rubbish heap.

Fungus grew, mushrooms and toadstools appeared with multiple popping noises, mould spread like gathering fog, maggots and beetles munched and the rubbish pile rapidly began to crumble and melt away. Then the Crone sent in the worms, and it turned into soil. A rich, rotting smell arose.

"Pooh!" said Rosie cheerfully, wrinkling her nose. "That's better than the other stink!"

"It's beginning to get muddy!" Rowan lifted first one boot and then the other. "I think we'd better get back, or we might sink!"

The Crone turned, her dark eyes gleaming. "I should if I were you. This was once marshland, you know," she advised, with a flash of white teeth.

They backed off hastily, as the mud began to rise.

"Exit that way!" Nubitha had gasped, and that was all any of them said, putting all their energy into escape.

Holly had drawn ahead of the others as they ran.

Nearly there. Just around the corner was the exit. Their

feet were slipping on the floor.

"*Mud?!*" exclaimed Yarris. "What's mud doing inside?"

They had no time to think about that, they had to keep running. Nearly there, thought Holly.

"Let go!"

Holly turned to see Yarris and Nubitha, struggling in the arms of the guards. They had been caught.

"Yarris! Nubitha!"

"Run, Holly! Get away!" yelled Yarris

"Get help – tell people outside what's going on!" called Nubitha.

"Shut up! You'll never get out of prison for this!" snarled the guard.

Holly darted around the corner – out of sight of the guards.

But not out of sight of another corridor, which was occupied by one of the least welcome people there – Vectira, the spiteful girl from Holly's class, immaculate in the most fashionable pink clothing.

"*There* she is!" shrilled Vectira, pointing. "Guards! Over there! *Get* her!"

CHAPTER TEN

Vectira's voice was loud and shrill. Holly knew the guards would hear. Once they came, Holly would be caught for sure. She had to do something.

In desperation, Holly bent down, grabbed a handful of mud and flung it at Vectira. It hit, splattering her chest, face and hair.

Vectira squealed indignantly. *"Oh!* My clothes! Oh! The *mess!"* She wiped silvery make-up from her face with her hands, revealing brown skin. Then, to Holly's amazement, her face changed, the malice fading away. Her violet eyes became wide and wondering. She lifted her hands and sniffed them. "My hands... soil...I remember...I used to have my roots in the soil... my name was... Violet..."

Holly paused, panting, astonished. "Violet?"

"Yes. I was the elf of the Violets. What *happened* to me? I've been mad, wasting my life, starving myself! When what I really want to do is… dance barefoot on the grass! In the rain! Yes!"

Holly gaped at her, but there was no time. She had to get away, to get help. "Come on!" She ran towards the exit, leaped at the door, pounded on it, pushed it – and it gave way.

"Oh, look! Run *quick*, all of you!" urged Rosie.

"The animals!" exclaimed Rowan.

A party of elves had been sent to find and free the squirrels, rabbits and chinchillas from their cages. Now a crowd of small furry animals came hopping, darting, scampering hastily across the mud. The weaker ones were being carried by the elves – Meadowsweet and Reed had so many squirrels clinging together on their heads and shoulders that they looked as though they were wearing very unusual hats. They staggered under the weight as they skipped from one patch of earth to another, like stepping stones. Some of the elves weren't wearing the normal tunics – there were two in the uniforms of Mall guards, and three wearing grey robes with the hoods down.

"Some from inside the Mall helped them!" realised Rowan. "Oh, I wonder if those elves – Holly and Thistle – I wonder if they're there?"

"Yeah," agreed Rosie, "They might be!"

"Made it!" exclaimed Reed.

Squirrels showered down from the elves onto the grass that had sprung up and spread out from the feet of the Three. Rabbits paused to clean their paws and whiskers, then began nibbling the grass. The wood and flower and river elves were welcoming the Mall elves, who looked dazed. Three chinchillas made for Misty, and they greeted each other with exclamations of ecstasy and sympathy. The air was soon full of high-pitched chattering, and one phrase began to stand out.

"Hungry! Hungry! Hungry!"

Misty went running up to the Mother. "Mother," she began, dipping her head and whiffling her whiskers, then gazing up at her with hopeful eyes. "We are hungry, hungry, hungry! Any – perchance – any hazel nuts?"

The Mother laughed. "Hazel," she said – and an elf with brown skin and green eyes turned around.

"Yes, Mother?"

"Hazel, please would you provide your bounty for these, our hungry children?"

"Certainly, Mother," replied Hazel with a smile and a bow. She opened her hands and hazel nuts poured out, bouncing on the grass.

With eager exclamations of delight, the squirrels and chinchillas pounced upon them, held them in their paws, and tucked in. The cries of "Hungry!" were replaced with, "Mm! Tasty tasty tasty! Thank you, Hazel! Thank you, Mother!"

Rowan turned back towards the rising mud with a smile on her face – the furry animals were so funny and cute!

But her smile dropped away.

Something was rising from the mud. Something round, something head-sized. She gasped.

"What?" asked Rosie, then, "Oh! What is *that?*"

"I don't know." Rowan couldn't keep her eyes off it. It was moving from side to side, as though blindly searching for something.

"A giant worm?" suggested Rosie. The head was being followed by a writhing body. Then two arms flung themselves out. "Not a worm, then," amended Rosie. "It's a person!"

Rowan had noticed something that made her shudder. She could see, even beneath the coating of mud, that the hands had bright red fingernails.

It was the body she had seen earlier.

Zombies! she thought, gulping. And the thing was wriggling up out of the mud, would soon be free, would be able to get at them. "Rosie," she began, trying to keep her voice steady as she backed off, "I think we ought to move away…"

Rosie stayed put. "I just want to see!"

"Rosie! Look, I think it's a – a zombie!"

"Well, it is nearly Halloween! Let me *see,*" insisted Rosie, even though Rowan tugged at her arm.

"It's an elf!" declared Rosie in a triumphant voice.

The elf had opened its bright green eyes. Its hair was cream. It leapt up out of the mud, flinging its arms wide so the bright red fingernails flew off and scattered like autumn leaves. "I am Clover!" she declared. Already, round green leaves and cream-coloured flowers were gathering around her body to form a tunic.

Rowan sighed with relief.

"Clover!" cried Meadowsweet, holding out her arms. "Welcome back! It's been so long!"

Clover skipped over the mud, to be embraced and welcomed by the other elves.

Rosie's brown eyes were wide. "Wow! That's amazing!"

"Yeah, it's totally amazing," agreed Rowan, full of gladness.

"Rowan?" There was a tentative voice. "Rosie?"

They turned around.

It was Holly.

Holly and Violet had stumbled outside, gasping and blinking in the sunlight. Smells rose to their nostrils, not chemical ones, but earth, soil, plants. Mud squelched underfoot, instead of the rubbish heap that Holly expected. Beyond the mud was grassland.

And there were elves all around, clad in leaves and flowers rather than tailored fashions, their feet bare rather than shod in high-heels, their skins brown and golden rather than silver-white. All of them had determined expressions.

Holly and Violet blinked, bewildered.

"What now?" asked Violet.

"We…" began Holly, momentarily at a loss.

At that moment, dozens of small furry animals appeared, some carried by elves, scurrying and hurrying across the mud to the grass. Holly's heart leapt as she saw guard uniforms, and attendant ones. Once they'd reached the other side, her eyes scanned them eagerly.

But, no. Yarris and Nubitha weren't amongst them.

However, she had noticed her cousins. And the Three. Maiden, Mother, Crone, the three goddesses…

Somehow she didn't want to face them immediately.

She would go for the safer option.

"Come on, Violet. We're going to meet my cousins," she announced.

"So you remembered who you were because you had mud thrown on you?" asked Rowan.

"That's right," agreed Violet.

"*Everyone* needs to remember! We need to *hurry,*" insisted Holly, who felt they had wasted far too long explaining what had happened already. "Look – I'll prove it! Lagana – it is Lagana, isn't it?" she asked one of the grey-robed elves. "You were in the rebels. We met before."

"Yes. That's what they call me," agreed Lagana, who had bright blue eyes.

"Excuse me a moment." Holly scooped up a handful of mud, and then smeared it onto Lagana's face.

There was a pause. Mud slid slowly down Lagana's cheek and dripped onto her robe. Two lumps of it detached themselves and dropped onto the grass. Rosie giggled.

Then Lagana blinked, and looked around, as though waking up from a dream. "I am… I am… Forget-me-not!"

"Forget-me-not? You *did* forget!" pointed out Rosie with a grin.

"Rosie! Hush, it's not funny," whispered Rowan.

"I did forget," agreed Forget-me-not. "But I never will again! I know who I am now!"

"See?" Holly turned around, appealing to the Three, who were watching. "It works! We have to wake them up! They've got Yarris and Nubitha! They're holding them prisoner! And Zest too. We have to get mud on them!"

Rosie chuckled. "Throw mud at 'em? Sounds like fun to me!"

"Fun?" Holly paused, frowning doubtfully. "It's just something we have to do."

"But how to we *get* to them?" asked Rowan, practically.

"That is not a problem," said the Crone, with a smile and one raised eyebrow. "The Mall is sinking. They shall have to escape. We shall be ready, that's all."

"But the people in prison," began Holly.

The Mother turned to survey the elves. "Ivy," she spoke, and an elf whose hair was dark green with a pale streak of cream stepped forward.

"Yes, Mother?"

"We need you now."

"Certainly, Mother. If the rest of you would stand back."

The Three stood in a triangle around Ivy. The elf closed her eyes. Her lips began to move, muttering incantations. A glowing green aura gathered around them. Everyone felt a sense of gathering power. The earth began to tremble – and then, suddenly, green shoots sprang from the ground. Sprouting leaves as they went, they shot towards the Mall like streamers from a party popper. They spread rapidly over the concrete walls, wriggling, burrowing, digging. Cracks began to move outwards. The Mall began to crumble away under the onslaught. Pieces of the roof dropped away. For the first time, sunlight fell upon the inside of the Mall.

"Be ready," said the Crone.

Inside the Mall, all was confusion. Mud was rising. The walls were crumbling. Attendants were refusing to serve. Workers were refusing to work. The very Mall itself was sinking. There was only one option – escape!

To the sound of alarms, and hysterical screams, the Mall elves began to stream like brightly-coloured fluttering litter caught in a breeze, down the corridors towards the doors to the outside which were not usually opened.

To the doors, where Rowan, Rosie, Holly and the elves were waiting for them, their hands loaded with dripping balls of mud.

"You were right, Rosie!" gasped Holly as she bent, scooped, flung, bent again for more mud to keep up the barrage against the outraged, fleeing inhabitants of the Mall. "This *is* fun!"

"You bet!" agreed Rosie. "Ha! *Got* him!"

"Ten points for you!" laughed Holly.

"Oh, *nearly!* The shoulder instead of the head! I'll get her in a moment!" Rowan scooped mud, wound back her arm and threw in a way she had learned when Daddy Taylor taught her how to bowl in cricket. She wondered briefly what he would think of the use to which she was putting her skill… "Howzat!" she cheered, flinging her arms up – the mud had hit her formerly elegant target right on the nose.

"Yay!" approved Rosie and Holly. Holly was exhilarated – she was particularly proud of hitting one of the judges who had failed her full in the face, sending splatters of muddy water all over her clothes and knocking her elaborately curled high-piled wig off. It fell with a splatch into the mud.

"Looks like a dead mop!" giggled Rowan.

"It does! It does!" Holly yelped with laughter.

"Holly!"

Holly looked up, surprised, to see Yarris and Nubitha scrambling down the crumbling wall of the Mall towards her, using the ivy to hold on to.

"You're free! Oh, fantastic!" she cried, pausing in her onslaught, her hands dripping mud.

"The ivy," they explained. "It pulled the roof off!"

"We grabbed onto it and climbed out!"

"All the prisoners are escaping!"

"The ivy strangled the machines!"

"And the advert screens!"

"Brilliant!" Holly's blue eyes shone with delight. "Everybody – this is Yarris and this is Nubitha – they've been organising the rebels. They've been fantastic!"

"Pleased to meet you," said Rowan politely. "I would shake hands, but..!" She smiled, holding up her muddy dripping palms.

"Hello!" Rosie grinned fiendishly. "Stand very still now, and take your medicine!"

"Rosie, no!"

But it was too late. Splat! went the mud onto Nubitha's face. She gasped, wiped it, blinked in the now familiar

110

awakening. Then she laughed. "I'm Thistle!" she cried. "I remember now!"

"Oh, yeah!" realised Holly. "Spiky purple hair like thistle flowers! It goes!"

"Everybody's been looking for you," began Rowan.

But Thistle bent, scooped up mud, grinned at Rosie, "I'll get you!"

"Eek!" Rosie ducked and covered her face as the mud ball flew over, missing her – but catching Meadowsweet in the middle of the back.

Meadowsweet turned around and exclaimed, "Thistle! There you are! How I've missed you!"

"Who are you, really?" Rowan asked Yarris. He shook his head. "I don't know. But I'm going to find out. No -" holding up a hand and smiling at Rosie. "I'll do it myself." He bent, scooped, took a deep breath and then ducked his face into his open palms and the mud.

They watched. He smiled, beneath his covering of mud, his dark green eyes lighting up. "Holly!"

"Yeah?" asked Holly.

"I *am* Holly!" He spread his palms.

"Er, *I'm* Holly," said Holly carefully, thinking perhaps he had been confused by the mud.

"I'm Holly too! I am the elf Holly!" He laughed. "See!" And he began wrestling himself out of his guard's outfit, pulling off his boots, undoing his jacket and flinging it off. Holly the girl's eyes widened and she backed off a little, not wanting to see a male elf undress. But, by some magic, Holly the elf now had a tunic of dark green spiky leaves, a belt of

111

woven holly twigs and a necklace of bright red berries. His bare dark brown feet beat a tattoo of joy on the grass. He took Holly the girl's hands, swung her round, then flung his arms around her for a swift strong hug.

Gasping with a mixture of pleasure and embarrassment, Holly watched her namesake elf running from one elf to another, greeting, welcoming, laughing. And then they saw him approach the Three, Maiden, Mother, Crone, bowing to each.

"My holy son, holy tree," said the Mother, placing a hand upon his shoulder. "Tinne, your true name. You have done well."

"Not that well. I forgot."

"And yet you continued with the struggle, even though you did not remember who you truly are."

He nodded. "I was not alone. Many played their parts. Thistle – Zest – Holly the girl – others."

"That is true. Yet you are one of the sacred tree elves, one of the months, so your responsibility is greater than theirs. And it is not over yet."

"Very true," he agreed.

Then Holly the elf joined Holly the girl, and Thistle too, and all the others, enthusiastically pelting the escapees with mud, until everybody was so covered they couldn't tell who had been who.

"Wish we would get *him*, though," remarked Holly the elf, gesturing upwards.

They all became aware that above them in the sky, the Pod was buzzing around like a bluebottle. Inside it was the Boss, watching the ruin of his empire.

Finally, the Crone raised her arms, and bade them all stand well back.

The Mall sank beneath the mud with vast glupping bubbling sounds. The surface rose in a bubble which swelled bigger and bigger, then finally exploded, flinging wet, aromatic mud all over everybody. They hadn't been standing quite far enough back.

Holly gasped, blinking. She wiped mud from her eyes with the back of her hand.

"Holly, are you all right?" asked Rowan. "Your *clothes!*" she added sympathetically, knowing that these things mattered to Holly.

"That's all right – mud packs are good for the complexion!" replied Holly in a shaky voice. Then she began to laugh.

And then she began to sob, and stumbled over to her cousin. Rowan put both arms around her, hugged her and patted her back.

"That," said Rosie, shaking her head slowly and grinning, "was *beyond* amazing!"

"And now for the healing," said the Maiden. She raised her arms to the sky and sang. Clouds gathered, there was a single drop of water, then another, then a pattering, and down came the rain. Not cold, unpleasant rain, but warm fat drops like summer. Everyone lifted their faces to it, like flowers do to the sun. Water slid down their faces, their hands and arms, their bodies and legs, washing them clean again. It felt wonderful.

113

Afterwards, the Maiden raised her arms again, singing another song. The clouds cleared, the sky was bright blue, newly washed. And the sun shone golden, its warm touch a blessing on them all.

"It's still a mess," observed Holly the girl, looking at the vast stretch of mud with here and there a strand of tangled ivy.

"Sh, they're doing something," whispered Rowan.

The Three gathered in a triangle around the Crone's cauldron, which began to glow green.

"Seed and shoot," began the Maiden.

"Rich fertile earth," said the Mother.

"Transformation!" cried the Crone.

Suddenly there was an uprush of water, and someone huge and green and leafy sprang up out of the cauldron and landed on the grass. "Ho, Goddesses! I live again!" he bellowed joyfully.

"It's the Green Man!" cried Linden.

"God of the forest!" added Holly the elf, smiling.

The Green Man's skin was greeny-browny-greyish like the bark of an oak tree, his tangled mossy beard was bright green, oak leaves and twigs sprung from his head and body, and his eyes were acorn greeny-brown. When he spoke, his voice was a deep rumble, and it seemed that all the earth and grasses trembled, not from terror, but from respect.

"I am the Green Man! The spirit of the forest, the guardian, the god!"

"He's a bit like Daddy Taylor," said Rosie, thoughtfully.

"Not quite. I mean, he's hundreds of years old, so he came first… you know," said Rowan, "Daddy Taylor's a bit

114

like him!"

"Yeah!" agreed Rosie. "So's Dad."

"Yeah."

"We need to restore the woodland," said the Maiden, taking the Green Man's hand.

He nodded his leafy head, then looked up, surveying the elves. "A berry or two, Holly," he rumbled.

Holly the elf went to him, took off his necklace and held it out in both hands. The Green Man plucked the bright red berries.

"And a hazelnut or two." Hazel picked the nuts from her necklace.

"Now." The Green Man held out his massive hand, and put the berries and nuts into their upturned palms. "Take these with you, and scatter them everywhere you can."

"Mm! Hazelnuts, crunch, crunch, crunch, yum yum!" chattered Misty eagerly, leaping onto Rosie's shoulder and reaching out both front paws.

"No, Misty! Don't eat it!" protested Rosie.

"Smells nice!"

"You would regret it," said the Green Man, wrinkling his eyes and cheeks into a smile. "It would spring up into a bush in your insides and burst that little tummy of yours like a bubble!"

"Eek!" squeaked Misty, alarmed, dashing from Rosie's shoulder. Everyone laughed.

"Have one of my own hazelnuts," offered Hazel.

Misty eyed the proffered nut warily.

"Go on - to recover from the shock!" urged Hazel. "It's safe!"

Misty took the nut, held it in her paws and nibbled. "Mm-mm!" she munched, "Tasty, tasty, tasty!"

Everyone laughed again. "Takes more than a bit of a scare to put you off hazelnuts, Misty!" said Rowan.

"True, true, true!" agreed Misty.

"Come on, Holly!" Holly the elf smiled at Holly the girl, and filled her hands with holly berries. "We'll make things grow again."

"But it'll take years, though," she said regretfully.

Holly the elf winked at her. "Don't you believe it!"

The Green Man called the tree elves forward one by one. Soon everyone's hands were full of acorns, nuts and seeds of various kinds.

The first one to plant an acorn was the Green Man himself. He bent down and poked it into the mud with one finger, then stood back. For a moment, nothing happened. Then a little green shoot popped up. It began to grow taller. Leaves unfurled from the top, little branches, then bigger ones as the trunk thickened. The leaves flapped like butterfly wings as the tree grew taller and taller. Finally it stopped, the leaves turning dark green, then brown, with acorns on the twigs – normal for this time of year.

"Wow!" Holly's jaw dropped. "Awesome!"

"You see?" Holly the elf bent and planted a bright red berry. They both watched as a little shoot grew to a small but thriving holly bush, covered in red berries.

It was great fun, making the forest grow again. Oaks, beeches, lindens, hollies, hawthorns, hazels, alders and willows – all kinds of trees grew as the girls and the elves skipped around, planting and scattering, never tiring of watching the miracle of life. The squirrels took the opportunity to scamper up the trees and gather twigs and nuts for nests and food.

Meanwhile the Maiden and other elves were restoring the meadow and the marshland. Flowers appeared in between the green grass stalks – creamy-white clover, golden-yellow buttercups, and daisies like little suns with yellow hearts and white petals. Reeds sprang up on the marshy ground and around the ponds, joined by bright blue forget-me-nots, creamy meadowsweet, pinky-purple mallows and golden marsh marigolds. The flat plate-like leaves of water-lilies floated on the green surface of the ponds, with their bowl-shaped flowers as white as new snow. Here and there, frogs appeared, some sitting on the water-lily leaves to catch flies, others jumping into the ponds with plopping sounds. Fish and newts swam in the water, little flotillas of black moorhens and speckled brown ducks on top of it. Dragonflies buzzed, their bodies as blue as kingfishers, their wings iridescent rainbows like bubbles.

Soon the air rang with the happy songs and calls of birds, croaks of frogs, chattering of squirrels and chinchillas, laughter and song of elves and humans. The land was restored, with all the normal creatures that had been there before the Mall had begun.

"You think you've won?"

They looked up. The shiny Pod was still circling around. The Boss's contemptuous face could be seen through the windscreen. His voice was broadcasting from a microphone.

"You haven't won! The minute you lot are gone – you silly ugly women, you stupid leafy hippy man – I'll start again! You can't beat the entrepreneurial spirit! You can't stop progress! You can't stop me, you can't, you – oh *sugar!*" Too late, he realised that he had been so busy shouting at them he hadn't been looking where he was going. With a horrible crunch, the Pod crashed straight into the oak tree that the Green Man had planted, ricocheting from one branch to another, then wedging itself firmly in the fork of the tree.

"Ooh! Is he going to be okay?" wondered Holly the girl.

"Never mind *him*, what about the tree?" asked Rosie.

The Green Man looked at her and laughed. "The tree is fine, young sister. I shall fetch this man down."

This he proceeded to do. The Boss stood in front of him, defiant in his fine suit, his hair ruffled. Everybody fell silent, watching him.

"And now," announced the Mother, "to deal with this man who calls himself the Boss."

"Hang on. How did the Boss ever get in here?" wondered Rowan. "He's a grown man! He's too big. How would he fit?"

"Ah, he first came to Nuin Duir when he was thirteen," began the Maiden. "Short for his age. He was a lonely boy, highly intelligent with a brilliant scientific mind. His parents were selfish, and barely cared for him. He was sent to various crèches as a baby, then to boarding school when he was just six years old. He was physically weaker than the other boys, but used his intelligence to manipulate them and escape their bullying. He chose to use his intelligence for selfish ends rather than good."

"Why shouldn't I look out for myself?" snapped the Boss, deeply discomfited at being exposed in this way. "It's a dog-eat-dog world, you know! That's just how the world works."

"But it isn't," protested Rowan, who couldn't help feeling a bit sorry for him in spite of her anger. She knew what it felt like to be bullied. "There are always people being kind to each other, and making friends, and co-operating!"

"Sentimental nonsense!" snorted the Boss. "There are winners and there are losers. *I'm* a winner."

"Not any more you're not!" said Rosie, who didn't feel in the least sorry for the Boss.

"One day," continued the Mother, "he was in pursuit of a beetle, because he wanted to kill it and implant a small computer inside it, to create artificial life. The beetle went through a hollow oak just outside the school grounds, and he followed."

"How do you know all this?" demanded the Boss. "Nobody knows this!"

"We know all the memories and actions of those who come to our world. We are Goddesses, after all." The Mother smiled, then continued. "Now, there is a certain vibration, a certain resonance necessary to travel from your world to this. He realised this, and then dedicated the next few years to creating a machine to replicate this resonance – for he did not want to have to go through the hollow tree each time."

"Indeed I didn't! Me? Crawl like a worm? I don't think so. I made my machine." The Boss couldn't resist boasting. "And it worked too!"

119

"Yet coming here via a machine is a not a comfortable experience. It is not the same as the natural way. One might compare the vibration of beautiful music with the vibration of chainsaws cutting down great trees."

"Well, yes. It does feel rather like a buzz-saw going through me," admitted the Boss. "Shakes up every cell in your body. But worth it to get here and start my empire!"

"And now your empire is finished," said the Crone. "And you must accept the consequences of your actions. We are going to teach you a lesson."

The Boss held his chin high. "You can't do anything to me, you ugly, ridiculous old woman!"

The Crone raised one eyebrow. "You have caused too much suffering. You have caused many people to loathe their own bodies, to neglect and damage themselves, each other, and the earth, and to forget the natural balance of this world. You have been arrogant. You have thought yourself better than the earth – the earth that gives you life. Earth you are, to earth you shall return."

"What is she going to do?" whispered Holly the girl, wide-eyed. "She's not going to kill him, is she?"

"I don't know." Rowan shook her head. She still felt angry with the Boss, furious in fact. But the Crone was so powerful, and the thought of her actually killing the Boss gave her stomach-ache.

"You need to learn you are dependent on the earth, and not above it. Thus, I shall give you an appropriate shape to learn that lesson." The Crone raised both arms, opened her mouth and sounded out a deep note.

The Boss gasped, and clutched at this throat. His face went red. His eyes bulged. His suit crumpled.

"He's shrinking!" squeaked Rosie.

"His skin's changing colour." Rowan was glad he hadn't been struck down dead, but didn't know what was happening.

"Eww, it's going all lumpy!" Holly wrinkled her nose.

The Boss dwindled rapidly, his mouth became wider, his eyes bulged all the more, his head flattened and lost its hair, his suit crumbling away into nothing.

"Ooh, look look look!" Misty hopped excitedly from Rosie's left shoulder, onto her head, and then her right shoulder.

Now he was knee-high, now he was the size of a chicken, now the size of a potato…

"He's a *toad!*" exclaimed Rosie.

Rowan was open-mouthed with astonishment.

"Whoa! That is *awesome!*" whispered Holly.

The Green Man's loud, glad laugh rang out. "A toad! Bravo, my lady Crone! A wise and wonderful choice!"

The corner of the Crone's mouth turned upwards slightly, and humour gleamed in her dark eyes.

The toad looked utterly outraged, and croaked in indignation.

Rosie began to giggle. "Its *face!*"

"Rosie!" admonished Rowan, but she couldn't help smiling. It was so *appropriate* somehow, for the Boss to be a toad. In fact, the whole gathered crowd of witnesses began to laugh.

"Go on, toad. Into the mud," ordered the Crone.

The toad's expression changed to piteous. Its eyes bulged, pleading with them.

The Crone was implacable. "Go on."

"I'll do it." Rosie picked up the toad, and held it in front of her nose. "I hope you're ashamed of yourself!" she told it, sternly. Then she couldn't resist sticking her tongue out at it. It struggled in her hands, obviously resenting the indignity. She popped it quickly into the mud with a splatch.

The Crone looked down at the toad. "You stay there in the mud until you've learned enough, and then you're going back to your own world where you belong."

The toad squatted there in the mud, radiating resentment.

It was over.

CHAPTER ELEVEN

When Holly woke the next morning, back in the camp bed in Rowan and Rosie's bedroom, she felt quite different. For a moment, she wondered if it had all been a dream… But no. No dream could be so powerful. And when she lifted her hand to brush her hair from her face, she could smell earth, and flowers.

She remembered the wonderful feast: the purple blackberries, the smoky mushrooms, the crunchy hazelnuts, the sweet honey, the rosehip syrup and linden blossom tea. And the elves – oh, the elves! Thistle, and Holly and Violet, Linden and Beechen and all the other elves of meadow, marsh and pond, river and woodland. She had realised that *this* was true beauty – not make-up and fashionable clothes – but nature, flowers, trees, leaves, the natural colours of skin and hair and eyes.

123

Some of the elves chose to decorate themselves, but it was a celebration rather than a disguise. They made necklaces and bracelets of leaves, berries and acorn cups, and garlands of flowers all the colours of the rainbow. Holly the girl, Holly the elf and Thistle had garlanded each other with daisies, buttercups, clover and forget-me-nots.

Some of the river elves painted each other's faces with clays that were russet red, tawny yellow and slate blue – not like make-up, but in swirls and spirals. Holly had loved that, and she and Rowan and Rosie had even painted each other's faces, then looked at their reflections in a nearby pool. Rowan had painted spirals on Holly's cheeks. Holly had felt so glad when Rowan had liked the spiral and the half-moon that Holly had painted and thanked her for it. Rosie had demanded a nose and whiskers, and pretended to be a chinchilla like Misty, holding her hands like paws and squeaking, demanding hazelnuts. That had made everybody fall about laughing – even Misty, after pretending shrill indignation.

Then they had all joined hands in a joyful dance, Holly, the elves, her cousins and the Three, the wonderful Goddesses…

Holly the elf had spoken to Holly the girl afterwards. "Your nature is Holly," he had said, looking at her with his dark green eyes. "You need challenges, fights in your life. And you need to understand which are the good fights, not just fighting for fighting's sake. You need to stay in balance, not waste your energies. Clear, focused, as straight as a spear."

Holly the girl had reached out her hand, and taken his dark brown hand and squeezed it. "I know," she had replied. "You helped me to see what I'm like. Who I am. Which isn't who I thought I was. And things I thought were important aren't really. And some things I thought weren't important *are*. And now I know that, I'm going to do something about it."

"Good."

Holly turned around, feeling a tingling around her body. It was the Three Goddesses, and the Mother was the one who had spoken.

Holly wondered how she could possibly have dismissed them as ugly. They were beautiful, and it was more than just their appearance. They were truly wonderful. "Goddesses," she began, and then wasn't sure what to say. That she was sorry. That she was determined. That she had changed.

The Maiden smiled at her, blue-green eyes very kind in her freckled face. "We know," she said simply.

Holly couldn't help but smile back. And she realised that the miserable, tight, angry feeling that she had felt ever since her parents divorced was leaving her. Like a fist uncurling, something relaxed inside her, relaxing into a kind of peace, a kind of sureness, a kind of love...

"Life is for loving," began the Mother, her voice as rich and deep as fertile soil.

"Life is for learning," said the Crone, tilting her head, her eyes bright as a bird and deep as the ocean. She uncurled one long finger. For some reason there was a green-and-yellow caterpillar on it. Holly's eyes widened and she smiled

125

in surprise.

"Life is for laughing!" said the Maiden, with a merry chuckle, as golden as her hair.

"Value your body," said the Mother, "for it is the home of your soul."

"From the moment you are born, you have your body. It is a wonderful gift, which will last for the rest of your life," said the Maiden. "It changes and grows, but it will always be with you, until the day you die."

"Do not fear death," began the Crone. "For it is a transformation." She closed, then opened her fingers, the caterpillar was a small brown chrysalis. She closed her fingers and opened them again - and a blue butterfly flew up into the sky. "But value your life, it is where you are now, and it is precious."

"I will," Holly promised. "I will."

Now, lying in bed back in her world, she remembered an argument between Uncle Robert and her Mummy once. Uncle Robert had said that the way most clothes were made was terrible, with the workers in other countries having to work long hours, with few breaks, for very little pay. Some of them weren't even allowed time off sick, or holidays. He said Fair Trade clothes were much better. Nadine had said that was 'impractical' and 'sentimental,' and 'in today's competitive world we have to cut costs.' Holly had agreed with her Mummy then – Uncle Robert was just being silly. But now she knew what it must be like for the workers making clothes for her Mummy's company. The kind of clothes that she herself wore… Those workers, their lives were precious too.

She turned on her side and looked over at her cousins. At that moment, Rowan shifted and sighed, and her eyes opened.

The two girls looked at each other.

Then Holly grinned. "I'm starving," she said. "What's for breakfast?"

Rowan grinned back, her green eyes sparkling. "Loads of things. I feel like I could eat an elephant!"

"Hm." Holly put a finger to her chin and pretended to ponder. "I think I'd rather make do with cereal and toast, myself."

" And home-made jam!" Rosie bounced out of bed eagerly, chucking her toy crab Sideways onto the pillow. "We've got raspberry! It's full of pips, but it's *lush!*"

It was time for Holly to go home. She had enjoyed the rest of her stay, especially Bonfire Night. They had lit a huge bonfire, and shared jacket potatoes, and hot soup, and hot ginger drinks. Daddy Taylor had played his drums, and they had all joined in the singing, watching the flickering orange light on each other's faces, and the sparks and smoke rising high into the night sky. Holly had realised afterwards that she hadn't once worried about the way she looked.

Now Nadine's car had just parked in the drive. She got out, and shut the door behind her.

"Mummy!" Holly ran towards her eagerly. Nadine smiled, feeling surprised and pleased that Holly was so glad to see her. At that moment, her mobile phone rang.

Holly stopped dead.

Nadine reached for the phone.

Holly's shoulders slumped.

Nadine swiftly switched the phone off, and put it back into her handbag. Then she held out her arms towards her daughter. Holly ran to her, and they hugged each other tightly.

Holly looked up. Nadine was surprised to see her blue eyes determined and shining with a new light in them. Her sulkiness was gone. "Mummy," began Holly.

"Yes," replied Nadine, wondering what new fashion or toy her daughter was going to wheedle out of her this time.

She was in for a shock. "Mummy can your company do Fair Trade clothes? Because it's better for the workers. You see," Holly took Nadine's hand and began to lead her inside, "they're people too. Just like you and me. And it's not fair they have to work long hours for low pay and no proper breaks, and no sick pay or anything. And anyway, lots of people like to buy from ethical companies, so you wouldn't lose any money."

What an extraordinary mind her daughter had, thought Nadine, as she sipped the tea her brother had given her, and her daughter elaborated on the plans. Clear and focused.

She really must spend more time with her.

Well, Rajesh at work was always hinting she needed to delegate more... And Sandy needed more of a challenge. She could set them both exploring contacts and prices and conditions for this Fair Trade idea...

Was she really going to change the way she ran her

128

business on an idea from her own daughter?

Well… why not?

Nadine smiled. "Holly," she began, "That's a very good idea. We can start on Monday - how about that?"

Bob and Jenny Meadows exchanged surprised glances as they saw Holly and Nadine hug each other tightly for the second time that day.

Rowan and Rosie exchanged glances too… but they weren't nearly so surprised.

Both of them wondered what would happen the next time they went to Nuin Duir…

Quirky Dragon - Beyond The Ordinary
Books by Philippa Drakeford

Have you read Book One in the Through The Oak series?
Doorway Through The Oak.
When Rowan and her half-sister Rosie crawl through the hollow oak, they find themselves in the magical land of Nuin Duir, where they meet Findolf the talking dolphin, Misty the chinchilla and Linden and Beechen the tree elves. But Rowan has a problem: she is being bullied at school by Maxine, who criticises her red hair, unfashionable clothes, and, worst of all, her beloved father.
Asking for help from the Ash Tree Goddess in the Sacred Grove, Rowan is sent on a mysterious Quest...

Coming soon:
Ivy Through The Oak.
Rowan and Rosie are celebrating Midsummer with their friends in Nuin Duir, where Rosie tells them what she has found out about the family who used to live in their house a hundred years ago, including a girl called Ivy, who was the youngest of eleven children.
Ivy befriends a lonely boy called Ashley and they find their way into Nuin Duir. But after the harvest, there is a terrible storm, and it seems the way in will be cut off forever.
That is when the present and past mingle, and Rosie has an idea...

About The Author

Philippa Drakeford has been creating stories since she
was a child, fuelled by an avid appetite for reading
a varied collection of books, which was encouraged
by her understanding parents and aided by excellent
public libraries. This love of reading has in no way
diminished as an adult.
"I am inspired to write about things that are beyond the
ordinary, touching on the magical and spiritual,"
says Philippa. "I was brought up as a Quaker, and have had
an interest in different spiritual traditions for a long time.
My stories tend to explore themes that fascinate me,
such as the effect of cultural expectations on people.
I love to 'get inside the head' of people from different times
and different cultures. I enjoy overturning stereotypes.
I love humour and have been known to produce some
excruciating puns. Nature is very important to me."
Philippa is an illustrator by trade and has worked for
prestigious titles, publishing houses and individuals.
Commissions include *No Other Blue*, poetry by
acclaimed poet and comedian Craig Charles
(Red Dwarf, Coronation Street); and award-winning
Inclusion In The Primary Classroom by Margaret Collins.

Published by Appleseed Press.

www.appleseed-press.co.uk
quirkydragon@yahoo.co.uk